MINDING

MY BLACK

ASS

BUSINESS

RAJAH E. SMART

Minding My Black Ass Business

Copyright © 2026 by Rajah E. Smart

Publisher's Note: This is a work of fiction. Names, characters, places, and incidents are a product of the author's imagination. Locales and public names are sometimes used for atmospheric purposes. Any resemblance to actual people, living or dead, or to businesses, companies, events, institutions, or localities is completely coincidental.

Ordering Information: Quantity sales. Special discounts are available on quantity purchases by corporations, associations, and others. For details, contact the publisher at the address above.

First Edition
ISBN: 979-8-9944964-0-4 (Paperback)
Cover design by Rajah E. Smart Interior layout by Rajah E. Smart
Printed in the United States of America

CHAPTER 1: THE FORTRESS & THE WAVE

Part I: The Audit

The fight didn't start with a scream. In the Ellison household, fights never started with screams; they started with notifications. Darius stood in the kitchen, the marble island cold under his palms. The Buckhead morning light filtered through the custom blinds, illuminating dust motes dancing over a bowl of organic lemons that no one was allowed to eat because they were for "staging."

He was staring at a credit card alert on his phone: **$450.00 – SUPREME, LITTLE FIVE POINTS.**

"Four hundred and fifty dollars," Darius said, his voice level. He didn't look up. "For a hoodie."

Sasha was arranging white hydrangeas in a crystal vase near the sink. She didn't pause. She snipped a stem with a sharp, decisive *click*.

"It's an investment piece, Darius," she said, her tone breezy. "Mike says the resale value is huge. It's basically a stock portfolio you can wear."

"He is sixteen, Sasha. He doesn't have a portfolio. He has a learner's permit and a C-minus in Economics." Darius looked up. The fatigue in his eyes was old; it was structural. "I'm canceling the card."

Sasha froze. She lowered the shears and turned slowly, giving him the look she usually reserved for customer service representatives who told her a coupon had expired—a mix of pity and lethal irritation.

"You are not canceling the card," she said. "You'll embarrass him."

"Embarrass him?" Darius laughed, a dry, sharp sound. "He spent a car payment on a sweatshirt to look cool on TikTok. Embarrassment is exactly what he needs. It builds character."

"Character," Sasha repeated, shaking her head. "You always do this. You try to parent them like it's 1995. You want them to have grit? We live in Buckhead, Darius. They don't need grit. They need networking. They need to fit the aesthetic."

"So I'm just the bank?" Darius asked. The question hung in the air, heavy and ugly. "I'm just the guy who funds the aesthetic?"

"You're the provider," Sasha said, turning back to the flowers. "Don't make it sound dirty. You like being the provider. It makes you feel big."

"It makes me feel used," Darius snapped.

"Oh, stop," she waved a hand dismissively. "You're in a mood because of the quarterly review. Mike is a good kid. He's *creative*."

"He's entitled, Sasha! And Bea? She asked me yesterday if I could hire a driver for prom because she didn't want to ride in a 'regular Uber.' They treat me like a logistics hub."

Sasha slammed the shears down on the counter. The crystal vase rattled.

"They treat you like that because you *act* like a logistics hub!" she hissed, her voice finally rising. "You don't talk to them, Darius. You audit them. You quiz them. 'How are your grades? Did you check the oil? What's the ROI on that hoodie?' You're not a father; you're a consultant."

The words hit Darius in the chest like a hollow-point bullet. *You're a consultant.*

"I'm trying to prepare them for the real world," Darius said quietly. "Because out there? Nobody cares about their aesthetic. Nobody cares if they're 'creative' if they can't solve a problem."

"This *is* their real world," Sasha countered, gesturing around the pristine, white-marble kitchen. "And you're the one who built it for them. You wanted them to have everything you didn't, right? Well, congratulations. They have it. Don't be mad at them for enjoying the life you paid for."

She picked up the vase, water sloshing dangerously near the rim. "Fix the transaction, Darius," she said, walking out of the room. "And fix your face. We have the dinner at the Caldwells' tonight, and I need you to look like you love us."

She disappeared around the corner.

Darius stood alone in the kitchen. The refrigerator hummed. The expensive coffee machine hissed. He looked down at his phone. The alert was still there. **$450.00.**

He didn't cancel the card. Sasha was right; he was the one who had built the cage. He just hadn't realized he was locking himself in with the animals.

He turned and walked toward his office. He needed the "Fishbowl." He needed the code. He needed a problem he could actually solve.

The Server Down

Darius sat in the Herman Miller Aeron chair, the mesh digging slightly into his thighs. The dual 4K monitors hummed with a low-frequency electric whine that only he seemed to hear. On the left screen: the code for the avocado supply chain algorithm, a blinking cursor waiting for his command. *If X, then Y.* On the right screen: a calendar that looked like a game of Tetris played by a sadist.

He stared at the code. The logic felt distant now. Like a language he used to speak fluently—Latin or C++—but had suddenly, violently forgotten.

His phone buzzed on the mahogany desk. It vibrated against the wood—a harsh, insect-like sound that made his molars ache.

Sasha (3:20 PM): The audio on the reel is weird. Can you look at it before I post? It sounds tinny.

Sasha (3:22 PM): Also, did Hector get water? He looks sweaty in the background of my shot. It's un-aesthetic.

Mike (3:25 PM): Actually, can you order pizza? The organic kind mom likes? With the cauliflower crust?

Darius stared at the notifications stacking up on the lock screen. He looked at the time. 3:26 PM.

In his mind, he ran the simulation. The "Prop" simulation.

If he stayed: He would open Adobe Premiere and fix Sasha's audio. He would text Hector to move his landscaping truck out of the frame. He would order the cauliflower pizza—thirty-eight dollars plus tip—and track the driver on the app. He would eat a slice over the sink while Sasha edited her caption about "mindfulness."

It was a perfectly functional life. It was efficient. It was successful. And it made him want to put his fist through the dual 4K monitors.

He didn't scream. He didn't throw the phone. He just picked it up. He held it in his palm. It was warm from the battery usage, alive with the demands of five different people. It felt like holding a grenade with the pin pulled.

He pressed his thumb against the side button and held it. *Slide to power off.*

He didn't just tap it. He swiped his thumb across the glass with the finality of closing a casket. The screen went black. The connection was severed.

The silence that followed was terrifying. For a split second, panic flared in his gut—a reflex honed by twenty years of being "on call." *What if there's an emergency? What if they need me?*

Then, the silence of the room rushed back in. *Let them figure it out,* the silence seemed to say. *Let the world stop.*

He put the phone in the center drawer of his desk. He locked the drawer. He stood up. He left the cursor blinking.

He walked through the mudroom, past the rows of perfectly aligned shoes, and stepped into the garage. He bypassed the vintage Porsche 911 Targa. He went to the Ford Expedition.

He climbed in. The seat was worn leather, shaped to his back. It felt like a sanctuary. He pushed the start button. The V8 engine roared to life. He hit the garage door opener, revealing the blinding, humid afternoon.

Sasha was in the driveway, posing near the hydrangeas. She heard the door. She turned. She saw the Ford backing out.

She smiled. It was her "camera-ready" smile. She waved. A little finger-waggle. She assumed he was going to get the pizza. She assumed he was going to the Apple Store to fix the audio.

Darius shifted into drive. He didn't wave. He didn't nod. He pressed the gas.

He watched her in the rearview mirror. She stood there for a moment, confused, her hand slowly lowering. Then, she turned back to the camera. The show had to go on.

Darius got on I-75 North, heading toward the airport. He reached for the radio, skipping NPR and the noise of the stock market. He plugged in the old iPod he kept in the console.

He scrolled. *John Coltrane. A Love Supreme. Part 1: Acknowledgement.*

The first notes of the saxophone hit him like a physical weight being lifted off his chest. He drove past the perimeter. He drove past the suburbs. He drove until the strip malls turned into pine trees.

He wasn't Darius Ellison, CTO. He wasn't "Dad." He wasn't "Babe." He was just a man in a Ford, driving away from the life he financed, with a dead phone and a live jazz record.

Part II: The Arrival

The road to the end of the world was unpaved. It was a jagged scar of packed dirt and gravel that wound its way deep into the throat of the Olympic Peninsula, flanked on both sides by Douglas firs so ancient and thick they seemed to swallow the light before it could reach the ground.

Darius Ellison drove the *rented* Ford Expedition slowly, the tires crunching over the uneven ground, a rhythmic popping sound that felt deafening in the stillness. He had passed the last sign of civilization—a rusted mailbox leaning precariously into a ditch—forty minutes ago. Since then, there had been nothing but the aggressive, towering green of the rainforest and the gray, bruised sheet of the sky.

The GPS on the dashboard had surrendered ten miles back, the screen simply displaying a floating blue arrow in a sea of digital nothingness.

Destination Reached.

He didn't stop immediately. He let the car roll forward another few feet, the gravel groaning under the weight, easing it into the designated patch next to **Cabin Two**.

It stood alone, anchored into the rocky soil like a modern bunker. It was a striking, severe structure of glass, steel, and dark timber, designed not to welcome guests, but to disappear into the shadows of the tree line. There was no welcome mat. No porch swing. It was a building designed for people who wanted to watch the world burn without being touched by the flames.

Darius killed the engine.

The silence that followed was violent. It wasn't the passive quiet of an empty room in Atlanta, where the hum of the sub-zero refrigerator or the distant wail of a siren always lingered at the edge of hearing, reminding you that life was happening elsewhere. This was a primordial silence. It pressed against the windows of the SUV. It felt heavy, wet, and absolute.

Darius sat there, his hands still gripping the steering wheel at ten and two. His knuckles were ash-gray, the skin pulled tight over the bone. He stared through the rain-streaked windshield at the cabin, his chest rising and falling in shallow, measured breaths. He felt like a diver who had gone too deep, too fast. The bends were setting in.

You are here, he told himself, the thought sounding foreign in his own head. *You actually left.*

He opened the car door. The air hit him like a physical blow—cold, oxygen-rich, and smelling intensely of wet cedar, decaying ferns, and ozone. It was a smell so old it made the air in Atlanta seem synthetic.

He stepped out, his boots sinking slightly into the damp earth, finding his footing on the literal edge of the continent. He grabbed his single leather duffel bag from the back seat. He didn't look back at the car.

He walked up the stone steps to the cabin door, punched in the code he'd memorized, and heard the heavy *thunk* of the deadbolt retracting. Inside, the cabin was cavernous. The ceilings vaulted twenty feet high, and the back wall was entirely glass, offering a view of the lake that lay half a mile down the slope. The water was steel-gray, motionless, disappearing into the mist. It looked like a mirror waiting to be broken.

But Darius didn't care about the view. He cared about the walls.

He dropped his bag on the floor—a loud *thud* that echoed in the empty space—and walked to the control panel on the wall. He found the switch labeled *Storm Shutters*.

He flipped it.

Outside, a mechanical groan shuddered through the structure. Heavy, thick slabs of timber began to slide out from the eaves, rolling down over the massive glass windows like eyelids closing on a corpse.

Chunk. Chunk. Chunk.

The view of the lake vanished. The gray light was choked off. The cabin plunged into a deep, womb-like darkness, lit only by the faint amber glow of the fireplace's standby light.

Darius stood in the center of the room, listening to the final click of the locks engaging.

He was sealed in. The world was locked out. The landscaper, the HBO password, the quarterly reports, the fake smiles for Instagram —they couldn't get through the wood.

He didn't unpack. He didn't turn on a light. He simply walked to the oversized leather sofa, sank into it, and for the first time in a decade, he closed his eyes and let the darkness hold him.

Part III: The Cacophony

Three thousand miles away, in Portland, Amara Lewis was not fighting. She was evaporating.

The breaking point didn't happen in a scream; it happened in a schedule.

Amara sat in her Range Rover in the driveway of her own home. It was 6:15 PM on a Tuesday. She had just finished a nine-hour shift at her private practice. She had spent the day absorbing the grief of a woman whose husband had left her for a Pilates instructor, and the anxiety of a teenager who was pulling out his own eyebrows.

She had held their pain. She had nodded. She had offered tools. She had been the vessel.

Now, she stared at her steering wheel. Her phone, mounted on the dashboard, pinged.

Carter: Did you pick up the dry cleaning? I have the board presentation tomorrow. I put the blue suit on the shared calendar.

Amara closed her eyes. The blue suit.

She remembered him putting it on the calendar. She remembered seeing the notification pop up while she was in a session with a suicidal patient. She remembered thinking, *I must remember the blue suit.*

But she hadn't.

Another ping.

Keela: Mom, where is my glitter eyeliner? I think you moved it when you cleaned my bathroom. I literally can't find it and I'm leaving in 10.

Another ping.

Marcus: There's no milk.

Amara looked at the house. The lights were on. It looked warm. It looked like the kind of home featured in magazines about "balance." But to Amara, it looked like a mouth. A giant, gaping maw waiting to consume her.

She knew exactly what would happen if she opened that car door.

First, Keela would come down the stairs, vibrating with teenage urgency, accusing Amara of "hiding" the eyeliner. Then Carter would emerge from his study, holding an empty wine glass, looking at her with that specific mix of affection and expectation. He wouldn't ask how her day was. He would ask about the suit. And when she said she forgot, he would sigh.

It was the sigh that killed her. It wasn't an angry sigh. It was a *disappointed* sigh. It was the sigh of a man who viewed his wife not as a partner, but as a faulty operating system. *Glitch in the logistics hub. Please reboot.*

Amara felt a vibration start in her chest. It was the "tuning fork" sensation. It was the physical manifestation of being touched, needed, and summoned too many times.

She looked at her hands on the wheel. They were shaking.

She wasn't a person anymore. She was infrastructure. She was the electricity that kept the lights on, the water that kept them clean, the calendar that kept them on time. And like all infrastructure, she was only noticed when she broke.

I am breaking, she thought. The realization was quiet, cold, and absolute.

She put the car in reverse.

She didn't cry. She didn't scream. She simply backed out of the driveway.

She drove to the nearest ATM and withdrew the daily maximum. Then she drove to the outdoor supply store twenty minutes before it closed. She bought a waterproof duffel bag, three pairs of wool socks, and a map of the Olympic Peninsula.

She didn't go back for clothes. She didn't go back for her toiletries.

She only made one stop. She drove to the doggy daycare where her own dog, Dung-chul—the Golden Retriever she had adopted before the marriage, the one who looked at her with eyes that actually saw *her*—was boarding.

She picked him up. He licked the salt off her cheek.

"We're going," she told him.

She got on the I-5 North. She threw her phone into the passenger seat. It buzzed and buzzed and buzzed—Carter, Keela, Marcus—a chorus of needs singing into the void.

She didn't turn it off. She let it die.

Half a mile away from Darius's fortress, separated by a dense, impenetrable thicket of spruce and rocky outcroppings that would take twenty minutes to traverse on foot, Amara pressed her forehead against the window of her Range Rover.

Cabin Three sat on a ridge, higher up than the others, overlooking the curve of the lake. It was isolated, the driveway nearly a quarter-mile long, winding away from the main dirt track. It was the last house on the last road.

Amara sat in the driver's seat, the engine ticking as it cooled. Her hands were still on the wheel, gripping the leather so hard her knuckles were white. She wasn't moving. She couldn't.

"Chul," she whispered. Her voice cracked, brittle as dry leaves. "We're here."

Next to her, Dung-chul whined softly. The big dog shifted, his collar jingling, and rested his heavy head on her shoulder. He pressed his weight against her, grounding her. The warmth of his fur, the solid, unasking weight of his head, was the only thing tethering her to the earth.

She forced herself to uncurl her fingers from the wheel. She opened the door and slid out. Her legs felt shaky, unstable, like she had just stepped off a boat in rough seas.

The ground was uneven, a carpet of wet needles and moss that sprang back under her boots. Amara walked to the trunk and popped it open. She stared at her luggage. It wasn't just a suitcase; it was an admission of defeat. She hadn't packed cute outfits. She had packed oversized wool sweaters, thick socks, and three books on trauma processing.

She hauled the bag out. Dung-chul bounded past her, sniffing a fern with the intensity of a bomb squad technician.

She unlocked the door to Cabin Three. It smelled of lemon oil and disuse. She walked straight to the back of the cabin, through the open-plan living area, and out onto the expansive wooden deck that cantilevered over the drop-off.

The wind up here was stronger. She looked out. The landscape was immense. The lake was a dark smudge below, hidden by the canopy.

And then, she saw it.

Far away. At least half a mile down the shoreline, separated by a gulf of gray mist, sharp rocks, and dark water. There was movement on the deck of the other cabin—**Cabin Two**.

It was just a silhouette. A dark shape against the gray wood of the structure. A man. He was standing at the railing, motionless, facing the water. Facing her direction.

Amara froze. Her stomach dropped.

Her instinct was to retreat. To duck behind the doorframe. She had come here to be the only person on earth. Seeing another human being felt like a violation.

But the figure didn't move. He didn't wave. He didn't call out. He just stood there, a tiny, dark anchor in the vastness.

Dung-chul trotted up beside her, sensing the spike in her cortisol. He looked out through the railing and let out a sharp, singular bark —a sound that echoed across the valley, bouncing off the water and the trees like a gunshot.

The silhouette in the distance turned.

Amara felt exposed. She didn't want to be polite. She didn't want to be "Dr. Lewis."

Slowly, reluctantly, as if the air itself was resisting her, she lifted her hand. It wasn't a friendly wave. It was stiff. Palm out. A stop sign.

I see you, the gesture said. *Stay over there.*

The silhouette stood motionless for a long beat. Then, slowly, the figure raised a hand in return. Just once. A brief, sharp acknowledgment.

Agreed.

The figure turned and disappeared inside the cabin. A moment later, Amara heard the faint, distant mechanical grind of shutters closing, echoing across the valley like thunder rolling in.

The man had sealed himself in.

Amara let out a breath she didn't know she was holding. Her shoulders dropped two inches.

"Good," she whispered to the wind.

She turned back to the cold, empty room, called for Dung-chul, and slid the glass door shut. She locked it. Then she deadbolted it.

She was finally alone.

CHAPTER 2: THE RESCUE

T he morning didn't break; it seeped in.

In Cabin Two, Darius Ellison woke up to a darkness so complete he thought for a terrifying second that he had gone blind or died.

There was no sliver of light under the door, no glowing red eye of a cable box, no ambient city glow filtering through sheer curtains.

The storm shutters were doing their job. He was sealed inside a wooden lung.

He lay still, listening.

Usually, his mornings were a sprint. The alarm at 5:30 AM. The mental download of the day's calendar before his feet hit the floor. The immediate, cortisol-spiked anxiety of the inbox. *Who needs me? What broke overnight? Did the server crash? Did the twins crash the car?*

Today: Nothing.

He checked his wrist. No watch. He reached for the nightstand. No phone.

He had left it in the kitchen junk drawer, powered down, buried under a stack of takeout menus for restaurants that didn't deliver this far out.

He sat up. The silence was delicious. It felt expensive. It felt like the kind of silence you usually had to die to achieve.

He walked to the kitchen in the dark, navigating by memory and the faint gray outline of the appliances. He made coffee—simple, bitter sludge from the machine the rental agency had provided. It wasn't the single-origin pour-over he made in Buckhead. It was diner coffee. It tasted like charcoal and freedom.

He took the mug to the leather sofa and sat. He didn't open the shutters. He liked the cave. He liked knowing that outside, the sun might be rising or the world might be ending, and he didn't have to witness either.

He took a sip. It burned his tongue. He welcomed the pain. It was the only thing on his schedule.

Then, the banging started.

At first, Darius thought it was a woodpecker. But it was too low. Too heavy. It was a rhythmic, frantic thudding against the solid oak of his front door.

Thump. Thump. Scratch. Thump.

Darius froze, the mug halfway to his mouth.

Irritation, hot and prickly, bloomed in his chest. He lowered the mug slowly to the coffee table. He had paid a premium for "aggressive seclusion." The rental listing had used the words *remote*, *private*, and *unreachable*. If this was the property manager coming to ask if he found the thread count of the towels satisfactory, Darius was going to demand a full refund and then burn the place down.

He stood up, tightening the drawstring of his cashmere joggers. He walked to the door, ready to unleash the specific, withering scowl he reserved for junior developers who missed launch deadlines.

He unlocked the deadbolt. He threw the door open.

"Look, I don't need—"

He stopped. There was no one there.

He looked left. He looked right. Nothing but mist, wet trees, and the overwhelming gray dampness of the Pacific Northwest. The air smelled of ozone and wet dog.

Then, a bark. Loud. Demanding. Entitled.

Darius looked down.

The Golden Retriever from yesterday—the one belonging to the woman with the "stop sign" hand—was standing at the base of the stone steps.

He was a wreck. His golden fur, which had been fluffy yesterday, was now matted with burrs and caked in black slime. He was panting, his whole body vibrating with a kinetic energy that seemed to rattle his very bones.

"You have got to be kidding me," Darius muttered.

He started to close the door. "Go home. Go find your mom. I'm closed."

The dog didn't retreat. He lunged.

The animal scrambled up the stone steps, his claws clicking frantically on the slate, and grabbed the cuff of Darius's expensive joggers in his mouth.

He *pulled*.

Darius stumbled forward, nearly losing his balance. "Hey! Let go! That's cashmere, you menace!"

The dog growled—a low, guttural vibration that traveled up the fabric and into Darius's ankle. He tugged again, harder, his eyes locked on Darius with a manic, unblinking intensity.

Move. Now.

Darius tried to shake him off. The dog held fast, drooling slightly onto the gray fabric.

"Jesus," Darius hissed. "Fine."

He stepped out onto the porch. The cold air slapped him instantly, soaking into his thin t-shirt.

The dog released him immediately, backed up three feet, barked sharply, and spun in a tight circle. He looked toward the trailhead—a dark, gaping maw in the tree line that disappeared into the dense forest—and barked again.

Darius stared at the dog. Then he stared at the dark woods.

The woman.

He remembered her face from the porch yesterday. The exhaustion etched into the lines around her mouth. The clear, desperate desire to be left alone. She wasn't the type to send a dog on a playdate. She was the type who probably had the same "aggressive seclusion" clause in her rental agreement.

"Is she hurt?" Darius asked the dog, feeling absolutely ridiculous for interviewing a Golden Retriever.

The dog barked—a sharp, affirmative sound that cracked the silence—and took off running toward the trees. He stopped at the edge of the clearing, looking back, waiting. His tail wasn't wagging.

Darius looked down at his socks. He looked back at his warm, shuttered cabin where the coffee was still steaming. He looked at the gray sky that threatened rain at any second.

"Unbelievable," he muttered. "I am on vacation. I am literally on strike."

He groaned, a sound deep in his throat. He went back inside, slammed the mug onto the counter with more force than necessary, and shoved his feet into his boots. He didn't bother lacing them tight; he didn't plan on being out long. He grabbed a hoodie from the back of the chair—a black tech-fleece that cost more than his first car.

"This better be good," he announced to the empty room. "She better be bleeding or on fire."

He stepped out into the mist, slamming the door behind him. The lock clicked.

He followed the dog into the green hell.

The trek was a disaster from the first step.

Darius hadn't done cardio in three years, unless you counted walking from the executive parking deck to the elevator bank. He lifted weights, sure. He could bench press his body weight. But this? This was different.

The terrain was a personal insult. It wasn't a trail; it was an obstacle course designed by a sadist. Slippery rocks hidden under layers of decaying leaves, exposed roots that tried to snare his ankles like tripwires, and low-hanging hemlock branches that whipped wet moss across his face.

He was sweating within five minutes. Not the good, detoxifying gym-sauna sweat. This was the cold, clammy sweat of a body in shock.

"Slow down!" he yelled at the dog.

The dog ignored him, but then walked close to him, where Darius noticed his tag. Taking it in his hand, he struggles to read the name. "Dung-chul, " he stutters. Dung-chul was relentless. Every time Darius slowed to negotiate a particularly treacherous patch of mud, the dog would stop, bark, and circle back, nipping at the air near Darius's knees.

Faster, you useless human. Faster.

"I hate nature," Darius wheezed, stepping into a puddle that submerged his boot in freezing slime. The cold water seeped through the leather, soaking his sock. "I hate trees. I hate moss. I hate dogs."

They walked for twenty minutes. It felt like a week. The incline increased, the ground becoming rockier and less stable. Darius's breath was coming in ragged gasps now. He was mentally drafting a one-star review for the rental agency, *Property not secure; local wildlife harassed me into a rescue mission; perimeter breached*, refining the adjectives in his head, when he saw the color.

A patch of dark blue against the brown and green forest floor.

The dog sprinted ahead, letting out a high-pitched yelp that sounded more like a cry.

Darius crested a small ridge, grabbing a sapling for balance, and looked down into the ravine.

She was lying in a heap at the base of a massive cedar tree, looking like a discarded pile of laundry. She was curled on her side, half-buried in the sword ferns. Her yellow raincoat was twisted around her, mud smeared across the back.

She wasn't moving.

Darius's annoyance vanished, replaced by a cold spike of adrenaline. He slid down the embankment, mud slicking the heels of his Italian leather boots, not caring about the six hundred dollars anymore.

"Hey!" he called out, breathless.

He reached her. She was conscious, but barely. Her eyes were squeezed shut, her face pale and slick with rain and sweat. A streak of dark mud cut across her cheekbone like war paint.

"Hey," Darius said again, dropping to a crouch beside her. "Can you hear me?"

Amara's eyes fluttered open. They were unfocused, glassy with shock. She looked at him, blinked, and then frowned. Recognition dawned slowly, followed immediately by mortification.

"You," she mumbled. Her voice was thick, slurring slightly. "You're... the neighbor."

"I'm the rescue squad," Darius corrected. He scanned her body quickly. No blood on the coat. No unnatural angles in the spine. But her right leg...

Her right leg was bent strangely, the boot wedged between two large roots.

"Did you fall?" Darius asked.

"I decided... to nap," she whispered, closing her eyes again. "In the mud. It's... a spa treatment. Very exclusive."

"Funny," Darius snapped. He was in management mode now. Assess the damage, fix the problem, get back to the coffee. "Stay awake. Look at me."

Amara opened her eyes. She looked angry. Not at him, but at the situation. At the weakness of it.

"I slipped," she said, articulating carefully, fighting the pain. "Hit my head. Ankle is... wrong."

Darius looked at the ankle. The leather of her hiking boot was tight against the laces. Even through the boot, he could see the that she may have a light sprain.

"Can you stand?" he asked.

"I don't know," she lied.

She tried to push herself up on her elbows. Her face went gray. A low, strangled sound escaped her throat, and she collapsed back into the ferns, gasping.

"Okay. Don't move," Darius commanded. He put a hand on her shoulder to keep her down. She was trembling—violent, rhythmic shivers that he could feel through her coat. She was going into shock.

Darius stood up and looked around. No signal on his phone. No road. Just the trail back to the cabins.

It was half a mile of rough, uphill terrain. He looked down at her. She was a tall woman. Solid. She wasn't a waif. This wasn't going to be like carrying Sasha and her purse across a puddle in a parking lot. This was physics. This was leverage.

"I have to carry you, but it doesn't look that bad. To be sure, I will carry you." Darius said. He didn't try to hide the reluctance in his voice. He sounded like a man staring at a flat tire in the rain.

Amara's eyes snapped open. "No."

"Excuse me?"

"I don't want... to be carried," she said, her voice trembling with humiliation. "I can walk. Help me up is all I need."

"Lady, look at your foot. It looks like a grapefruit inside a blender. You aren't walking."

"I am not... an invalid," she hissed. "I just need a shoulder."

"I didn't say you were an invalid, I said you were heavy. Or—you *will* be heavy. And my back is shot."

"Then leave me," she said stubbornly. "Send help."

"There is no help!" Darius shouted, his patience fraying. "It's me and the dog! That's the roster! Unless you want Lassie here to drag you by your collar, I am your ride."

She glared at him. He glared back. It was a standoff of two stubborn, exhausted people in the middle of a rainforest, steam rising from their bodies.

"Fine," she whispered, looking away. The defeat in her voice was worse than the anger.

"Great. Thrilled."

Darius bent his knees. "Grab my neck. And for the love of God, don't vomit on me."

He swept his arms under her legs and her back. He grunted—a loud, involuntary sound of exertion—as he lifted.

She was dead weight. He felt his lower back spasm immediately, a hot wire of pain shooting up his spine. He grit his teeth and stood up, swaying slightly as he found his center of gravity in the mud.

"Jesus," he muttered, adjusting his grip. "What do you eat? Bricks?"

"Shut up," she breathed into his shoulder. "Just drop me."

"Not an option," he grunted. "Let's go."

The return journey was a slow, anaerobic nightmare.

The first fifty yards were fueled by adrenaline. Darius moved with a deceptive strength, his boots digging into the soft loam, the dog trotting ahead like a proud scout.

Then, the incline started.

It wasn't a steep hill, but with an extra hundred and forty pounds in his arms, it felt like climbing Everest without oxygen. The adrenaline evaporated, leaving behind the cold, hard reality of his fitness level. His biceps began to scream. His lungs burned with the metallic taste of copper.

Sweat ran into his eyes. His footing slipped on every third step.

"Put me... down," Amara wheezed. Her voice was right at his ear. He could feel the heat of her breath against his neck.

"Shut up," Darius grunted. "If I put you down, I'm not picking you up again. We are committed."

He stepped over a rotted log, his boot sliding precariously on the wet moss. He tightened his grip on her thigh to stabilize them, his fingers digging into the wet wool of her coat.

He felt her flinch.

"Sorry," he panted.

"Just... don't drop me."

"I'm trying," he snapped. "You try being a backpack."

They made it another hundred yards before Darius's arms simply refused to cooperate. His muscles were trembling so violently that he thought he might drop her out of sheer failure.

"We stop," Amara said, sensing the tremor. "Sir. Stop. I mean, what is your name?"

"Darius," he replied.

"Darius, can you stop?"

It was the first time she had used his name. It registered in his fogged brain.

He didn't argue. He stumbled toward a large hemlock tree. He let her slide down slowly until her good foot found the earth, keeping his arm clamped around her waist to pin her against the rough bark so she wouldn't crumple.

They stood there in the damp silence, chest to chest, both of them heaving for air. Once they had collected themselves, he helped her to his residence, which was closer than her cottage.

Amara's face was the color of old ash. She was sweating, her hair plastered to her forehead. She looked up at him, her eyes wide and dark with pain.

"I think I'm going to be sick," she whispered.

"Don't," Darius warned, his head hanging low, hands resting on his knees as he tried to catch his breath. "Do not vomit on my boots. These are Italian leather. They are already ruined, but vomit is a line."

Amara let out a sound that was half-laugh, half-sob. She looked down at his mud-caked feet.

"You wore... Italian leather... to a rescue?"

"Your dog didn't give me much of an option."

"I didn't have time to change!" Darius snapped, wiping mud from his face with his sleeve. "Your dog didn't give me a window to accessorize."

"He's... a good boy," she managed.

"He's a menace. He has no respect for cashmere."

Darius stood up straight, testing his back. It held. Barely. He looked at the trail ahead. It wound upward, vanishing into the mist.

"We have a quarter mile left," he said, his voice flat. "Can you hop?"

Amara looked at the trail—a gauntlet of slick roots and mud. She looked at her ankle, which was now throbbing with a visible pulse. She shook her head. "No."

"Then we go again."

He stepped in. This time, there was no hesitation, but there was no grace either. He was purely mechanical. He grabbed her. She wrapped her arm around his neck, smelling of wet wool, rain, and fear. He hoisted her up.

A groan tore out of him—loud and animalistic.

"Sorry," he muttered through gritted teeth.

"Just walk," she breathed. "Just walk."

The walk became a blur of pain. Darius stopped feeling his fingers. He focused entirely on his feet. *Step. Don't slip. Step. Don't slip.*

He cursed the rental agency. He cursed the forest. He cursed the concept of being a "good neighbor." He cursed Sasha for making him buy the Peloton he never used.

Amara didn't speak. She buried her face in his neck, her body tense, trying to make herself lighter, trying to disappear.

Finally, the trees broke.

The angular, dark roofline of Cabin Two cut into the gray sky like a promise.

Darius staggered the last fifty feet. His legs were jelly. He kicked the front door with the toe of his ruined boot.

He didn't have a free hand to punch in the code.

"Code," he grunted.

Amara lifted her head. She looked at the keypad. "What is it?"

"One... nine... eight... four."

She reached out a shaking finger. *Beep. Beep. Beep. Beep.*

The deadbolt retracted with a heavy *thunk*. Darius kicked the door open and stumbled inside.

The transition was jarring. They crashed from the wet, cold chaos of the woods into the dry, cedar-scented silence of his fortress. The warmth hit them like a wall.

Darius didn't make it to the sofa. He bypassed the living room and collapsed onto the thick woven rug in the entryway.

He lowered her down as gently as his failing muscles would allow, but it was still a clumsy landing. She landed with a soft *whump*, and he collapsed next to her, sprawling on his back, staring at the high timber beams of the ceiling.

For a long minute, there was no sound except their breathing. Ragged, harsh gasps filled the room.

Dung-chul trotted in behind them. He shook himself—a violent, full-body rumba that sent a spray of mud and water across the floor, the cabinets, and Darius's legs.

Darius didn't even flinch. He just closed his eyes.

"Nice dog," he deadpanned to the ceiling. "Remind me to bill you for the cleaning."

"He likes you," Amara's voice came from the floor. It was weak, strained, but there was a thread of amusement in it.

Darius lay there for another beat, letting the floor support his spine. He was covered in mud. His six-hundred-dollar boots were destroyed. His cashmere joggers were snagged and ruined. His back was going to require a chiropractor and possibly a priest.

And the silence he had paid for was gone.

He turned his head to look at her.

Amara was clutching her ankle, her eyes wide and dark, watching him with a mixture of gratitude and wariness. The mud on her cheek had dried. She looked wrecked. She looked beautiful in a terrifying, raw way.

"Welcome to the fortress," he said dryly.

Amara didn't smile. She just let her head fall back against the rug.

"Don't let me die in here," she whispered.

"Not today," Darius said, closing his eyes again. "I'm too tired to dig a hole."

He groaned, rolled onto his side, and forced himself to sit up. The rescue was over. The siege had begun.

CHAPTER 3: TEA, BOURBON, AND THE BALLOT BOX (THE CULTURAL AUDIT)

Amara took another sip of the beige tea. She grimaced, a full-body shudder that started at her shoulders and ended at her throbbing ankle.

"This is a hate crime," she repeated, staring into the mug like it contained poison. "I want that on the record. If I die of a blood clot tonight, tell the coroner it was the Lipton that finished me off. It tastes like wet cardboard and despair."

Darius swirled the Pappy Van Winkle in his own mug, watching the amber liquid coat the ceramic. The firelight caught the glass, turning the bourbon into a dark, liquid jewel.

"You're in America now, lady. I'm sorry, what is your name? I don't want to keep calling you, lady."

"It's Amara and thank you for not calling me lady anymore," she replied in her British accent.

"Well, Amara, we prioritize speed over dignity. It's our national ethos in *Ameriker*." He took a slow sip, savoring the burn that started in his throat and settled warm and heavy in his stomach. "Besides, Lipton built this country. It's the tea of the revolution. It's supposed to taste like struggle. You want nuance? Go back to London. You want caffeine delivered with the efficiency of a drone strike? You drink the Lipton."

He leaned back in the armchair, stretching his legs out carefully so as not to disturb Dung-chul, who was currently snoring on his left foot. The dog was a dead weight, a warm anchor keeping Darius tethered to the rug when his mind wanted to float away.

"So," Darius said, shifting gears. "British. But living in the Pacific Northwest. That is a very specific, very gray Venn diagram of locations."

"I like the rain," Amara murmured, adjusting the ice pack—frozen kale—on her ankle. The bag crinkled loudly in the quiet room. "It matches my internal monologue."

"And the accent," Darius noted. "You have the kind of accent that makes insults sound like compliments. You just told me I committed a hate crime, and it sounded like you were reading a bedtime story to a corgi."

Amara managed a weak, tight smile. "That's the trick. It confuses White people. They hear the Queen's English and they freeze. They don't know whether to clutch their pearls or ask me to narrate a documentary about elephants."

Darius snorted. A genuine laugh this time. "I bet that plays well in Portland."

"Oh, it's a hit," Amara said, shifting her leg. "They love me. I'm a two-for-one special. I check the diversity box, but I sound like *Downton Abbey*. It makes them feel very cosmopolitan. Until I actually have an opinion. Then it's..." She deepened her voice, mimicking a concerned, NPR-listening liberal. *"Oh, Amara, you're so... aggressive. Are you angry? Is this about generational trauma?"*

Darius nodded slowly, raising his mug in a toast. "The 'Angry Black Woman' remix. Classic track. Plays on every station."

"Exactly," Amara sighed. "But with a twist of 'ungrateful immigrant.' They love an immigrant until you critique the plumbing. Or the healthcare. Or the fact that they put marshmallows on sweet potatoes."

"Hey," Darius warned playfully. "Don't come for the yams."

"It's candy, Darius. It's a vegetable behaving like a dessert. It's dishonest."

"It's joy," he corrected. "But go on."

Amara groaned, letting her head fall back against the sofa cushions. The fire popped, sending a spark up the chimney. "It's just... the politeness. That's the real difference between here and the UK. In London, the racism is like the fog—it's just everywhere, damp and chilling, but nobody acknowledges it. You walk into a room, and the temperature drops. They don't call you a slur; they just ask you where you're *really* from. Again. And again. Until you realize they're trying to locate the specific coordinate on the map where you belong, so they can mentally send you back there."

Darius laughed, a sharp bark of sound. "The Audit. I know the Audit. *'No, but where are your parents from?'*"

"Precisely," Amara said. "I tell them 'London,' and they look disappointed. Like I ruined the game. They want a hut, Darius. They want a village. They want me to give them a *Lion King* moment so they can feel worldly."

"See, that's where America wins," Darius said, taking a heavy swig of bourbon. "We don't do subtle. We do violence. In Atlanta, nobody asks where I'm from. They know where I'm from. I'm from the demographic they're trying to redistrict out of existence."

He gestured with his mug. "Here, it's the Sprint. Fast, aggressive, in your face. In the UK, it sounds like it's the Marathon. Endurance racism."

"It is," Amara agreed. "It's death by a thousand polite cuts. But at least in the UK, we don't pretend everything is 'awesome.' You Americans... you have this pathological need to wrap everything in glitter. You smile while you're dying. 'How are you?' 'I'm great! I'm bankrupt and my kidney failed, but I'm living my truth!'"

Darius chuckled darkly. "That's the brand. Optimism or death."

"And the politics," Amara said, the word coming out like a curse. "God, the politics."

Darius groaned, rubbing his temples. "Don't. I'm on strike."

"No, we have to," Amara insisted. "Because that's why we're both exhausted, isn't it? It's not just the kids. It's the noise. I look at my phone and I want to throw it into the ocean."

"Trash," Darius said, staring into the fire. "It's all trash. Red Team, Blue Team—it's just pro wrestling with nuclear codes."

"It's the same across the pond," Amara said. "We have the Posh Boys playing dress-up in Parliament, gutting the NHS while talking about the 'Blitz Spirit.' Nostalgia is a drug in England, Darius. We're addicted to the war. We keep voting for people who promise to take us back to 1945, forgetting that we were being bombed in 1945."

"And here?" Darius shook his head. "We got the Geriatric Ward. I look at Congress and I smell mothballs. You got one side explicitly promising to return to a time when I was three-fifths of a person— which, hey, points for honesty. I respect the hustle."

"At least you know where you stand," Amara murmured.

"Exactly. I know I'm the enemy. But the other side?" Darius's face hardened. "The 'Allies'? They're worse. They want to 'listen and learn.' They want to put a sign in their yard that says 'In This House We Believe' while they block the affordable housing zoning hearing three blocks over. They want my vote, but they don't want my neighbors."

Amara laughed, but it was a jagged sound. "The yard signs. Portland is paved with them. It's performative liturgy. It's the modern indulgence. I bought the sign, so I don't have to talk to the Black mailman."

"It's exhausting," Darius said. "I'm tired of voting for the 'lesser of two evils.' I'm tired of being told that if I don't donate twenty dollars right now, democracy dies on Tuesday. Democracy has been dying on Tuesday for twenty years."

"Your wife," assuming he is married, watches CNN all day, doesn't she?" Amara guessed.

"Religiously," Darius confirmed. "She thinks if she watches enough, she can manifest a policy change. I tell her, 'The server is corrupted. You can't patch this. You gotta wipe the hard drive.' She calls me cynical. I say I'm efficient. She listens to these same Blacks folks always running their flaps, and that's it."

"The Tavis Smiley types, if I get you. My husband, Carter, tries." Amara added, "Carter listens to podcasts at 1.5 speed. He thinks that if he understands the 'macroeconomic trends,' he can budget our way out of the collapse. He's optimizing the apocalypse."

They sat in silence for a moment, the weight of their shared fatigue filling the room. It was a specific kind of tired—not physical, but spiritual. The tiredness of being smart enough to see the cracks in the foundation, but too small to fix them.

"So what do we do?" Amara asked softly. "If it's all trash? If the Posh Boys and the Geriatrics are running the world into the ground?"

Darius looked at her. He saw the firelight reflecting in her dark eyes. He saw a woman who had carried the weight of the world's expectations for so long she had forgotten how to put it down.

"We mind our business," Darius said. "That's the revolution, Amara. We opt out. We stop trying to save a burning building and we just... sit on the porch. With every win they claim, we just simply respond, well, whoop-dee-doo."

"And let it burn, while I laugh at that statement?"

"Let it burn," Darius said, raising his glass. "We have marshmallows."

The Performance Review

Amara shifted on the couch, the frozen kale crunching under her ankle. She stared at the ceiling beams, tracing the grain of the wood with her eyes.

"It wasn't the politics that broke me, though," she said quietly. "It was the performance."

Darius looked over at her. "The Pivot?"

"More than that. The Pivot is reactive. You pivot when you walk into a room. The Performance... that's the maintenance. That's the upkeep."

She took a breath, her chest rising and falling slowly.

"Last Tuesday," she began, "I had a patient. A young woman. White. Very wealthy. She came in because she felt 'unfulfilled' in her marketing job. She cried for forty-five minutes about how hard it is to find 'authentic connection' in a digital world. I can't say I disagree and the idea of it."

Darius nodded. "Standard billable hour."

"Standard," Amara agreed. "But then she stopped crying. She looked at me. She wiped her eyes with a tissue I paid for, and she said, 'You're so lucky, Dr. Lewis. You're so... grounded. You have that *earth mother* energy. It must be nice to be so connected to your roots."

Darius groaned. "Oh no."

"Earth mother," Amara repeated, her voice dripping with acid. "She called me 'earth mother.' I have a PhD in Clinical Psychology. I wrote my dissertation on trauma response in displaced populations. But to her? I'm magical. I'm spiritual. I'm her mammy with a degree."

"What did you do?"

"I smiled," Amara said. The shame in her voice was palpable. "I smiled, Darius. I nodded. I validated her projection. I said, 'Thank you, that's very kind, because if I had said what I wanted to say— which was 'I am not your mother, I am not the earth, and I am certainly not your spiritual Sherpa'—she would have felt attacked. She would have written a review saying I was 'cold' or 'unrelatable.' So I performed. I let her consume me so she could feel better about her marketing job."

She turned her head to look at him. "I went to my car afterwards and I just screamed. No sound. Just open-mouthed screaming at the windshield. I realized I've been playing the 'safe Black lady' for 20 years. And I am so tired of being safe."

Darius stared into his bourbon. The liquid swirled, dark and heavy.

"I know the scream," he said softly. "I had a board meeting last month. The quarterly projection."

"The perpetual problem?"

"The very same. We were down four percent. Not a disaster, just a blip. Supply chain issues in Mexico. Standard stuff. But the CEO—Dave—he starts spiraling. He's pacing the room, talking about 'lean operations' and 'trimming the fat.' And then he turns to me."

Darius mimicked a deep, booming corporate voice. "Darius, you're good at navigating... sticky situations. You know how to talk to these people. Can you handle the vendors? You speak the language."

Amara winced. "He didn't."

"He did. 'You speak the language.' I don't speak Spanish, Amara. I took two years of French in high school. I speak Python. I speak Java. I speak C++. But to Dave? I'm Brown-ish. So I must know how to talk to the help."

"What did you say?"

"I said, 'Sure, Dave. I'll handle it.' And then I went home and deactivated my LinkedIn profile for three hours just to feel something."

He laughed, but it was a hollow sound.

"That's the Performance," Darius said. "It's being smarter than everyone in the room but having to act like you're just 'lucky' to be there. It's managing their ego so they don't feel threatened by your competence. It's knowing that if you make one mistake—just one—you're not 'having a bad day.' You're 'unqualified.' You're a 'diversity hire' who couldn't cut it. You know, Civil Rights causes White folks so many problems."

"And if you succeed," Amara added, "you're 'exceptional.' You're 'articulate.' You're a credit to your race."

"Exactly. You can't just be a guy who wrote good code. You have to be a symbol. And symbols don't get to take naps."

Amara looked down at her hands. They were trembling slightly.

"I think that's why I hate the jazz," she whispered. "Or why I thought I did. It feels like... exposure. It feels like taking the armor off. If I stop performing, if I stop being the 'earth mother' or the 'logistics hub' or the 'safe Black lady'... what is left?"

"You," Darius said.

"I don't know who that is anymore," she admitted. "I think she might be a bitch. I think she might be mean."

"She's not mean," Darius said. "She's just tired. And she has a sprain in her ankle. And she's drinking terrible tea."

Amara smiled, a genuine, soft smile that reached her eyes. "She really hates this tea."

"See?" Darius said. "That's a start. You know what you hate. That's the first step to knowing who you are."

He sat up straighter, the leather of the chair creaking.

"Tell me about your family, " he adds. "Simple like this, I have a wife named Sasha and two kids that get on my nerves," he says.

"Same—I have a husband named Carter and two kids that also get on my nerves."

"We spend our whole lives auditioning, Amara. For our bosses. For our spouses. For our kids. We're constantly trying to prove we deserve to be in the room. This cabin? This is the green room. The audition is over. You got the part."

"What part?"

"The part where you sit down," Darius said. "The part where you don't have to fix anything."

Amara looked at him. The firelight flickered, casting long shadows across the room. She felt a loosening in her chest, a physical sensation of a knot untying.

"You know," she said, "Carter thinks I'm here for a 'wellness retreat.' He thinks I'm doing yoga and drinking green juice. He texted me this morning: *'Hope you're finding your center.'*"

Darius snorted. "Sasha thinks I'm at a 'Tech Innovators Summit.' She thinks I'm networking with Elon Musk's cousins. She texted me: *'Make sure you tag the location. It's good for the brand.'*"

"They don't know us," Amara said, the realization landing with a heavy thud. "They live with us. They sleep next to us. But they don't know us."

"They know the performer," Darius corrected. "They bought a ticket to the show. They like the show. The show pays the mortgage. The show makes sure the dry cleaning gets picked up."

"And if we cancel the show?"

Darius looked at her. His eyes were dark and serious.

"Then they have to meet the cast. And they might not like the cast."

"I'm not sure I like the cast," Amara whispered.

"I like the cast," Darius said firmly. "The cast is funny. The cast hates Lipton. The cast plays a mean game of poker."

Amara felt tears prick her eyes again. She blinked them back, angry at her own vulnerability.

"You're good at this," she said. "The pep talk."

"I'm a manager," Darius shrugged. "It's what I do. I manage assets. And right now, you are a distressed asset. I'm trying to prevent a total liquidation."

"Thank you, I think."

"You're welcome. Now drink your tea. It's getting cold, and cold hate-crime tea is just tragedy."

Amara took a sip. She grimaced. "Still terrible."

"Good. Hold onto that hate. It's fuel."

Darius stood up, his knees cracking. He walked over to the turntable in the corner.

"Enough talking," he said. "We've audited the culture. We've roasted the government. We've deconstructed our marriages. Now, we need to address the real crisis."

"Which is?"

"The fact that you think jazz is anxiety set to music."

Amara groaned, throwing her head back. "Darius, please. Not tonight. I'm fragile." Darius goes to the crate of records he brought along.

"Fragile is exactly when you need Coltrane," Darius said, sliding a record from its sleeve. "You need to break so you can reset. Trust the process. Coltrane had this pain and you can hear it in the notes."

"I trust nothing," Amara muttered. "I am a skeptic. I am on strike."

"The strike is paused for a musical interlude," Darius said, dropping the needle.

The crackle of static filled the room, followed by the first, mournful notes of a saxophone. It wasn't frantic. It wasn't chaotic. It was slow. Deep. A sound that reached inside your chest and squeezed.

Amara stopped complaining. She listened.

And for the first time in twenty years, she didn't try to analyze it. She didn't try to organize it. She just let it hurt.

"To the cliff edge," she whispered to herself.

Darius sat back down. He didn't look at her. He let her have the moment.

They sat there in the Fortress, two runaways in sweatpants, watching the fire die down, letting the music fill the silence where the performance used to be.

CHAPTER 4: THE TOUCH (THE SHIFT)

Part I: The Siege

The storm didn't just arrive; it hunted them. For the next three days, the Olympic Peninsula ceased to be a landscape and became a gray, watery blur of violence. The wind didn't just blow; it screamed. It battered the heavy timber shutters of Cabin Two with a rhythmic, thudding intensity, like a giant fist trying to punch its way in.

Inside, the air pressure dropped so low it made their ears pop. The cabin, which had felt like a sanctuary, began to feel like a submarine taking on depth charges.

"It sounds like a velociraptor is testing the perimeter," Darius noted on the first night, staring at the front door as it rattled violently in its frame.

Amara, huddled under three blankets on the sofa, didn't look up from her Kindle. Darius recovered for her with Dung-chul. She felt comfortable in the clothing Darius provided, even though he brought some things from her cottage. "If a dinosaur breaks in, I'm tripping you. I have a bad ankle. I am designated prey. You have to be the sacrifice."

"That's cold," Darius said. "Practical. But cold."

"I'm British," she muttered. "We survive. It's what we do."

But underneath the banter, there was a genuine, creeping dread. The isolation was absolute. The road was gone—buried under a fallen hemlock that looked thick enough to crush a tank. The power flickered constantly, the lights buzzing like dying insects before plunging them into total darkness, only to zap back on seconds later.

And then there was the dog.

Dung-chul was not handling the apocalypse well.

If Darius was the stoic captain of this sinking ship and Amara was the pragmatic passenger, Dung-chul was the hysterical crew member who had realized there were no lifeboats.

The Golden Retriever spent the first hour of the storm pacing the perimeter of the living room, his claws clicking a frantic, staccato rhythm on the hardwood. *Click-click-click-click.* He would stop at the window, let out a low, vibrating growl deep in his chest, and then look back at Amara with eyes that were wide, white-rimmed, and filled with existential terror.

"He thinks the wind is a dog," Darius observed, watching Dung-chul bark at a particularly loud gust. "He thinks it's a giant, invisible Alpha dog challenging him for the territory."

"He's sensitive," Amara said, reaching out to stroke the dog's trembling flank as he passed. "He's an empath. He's absorbing the atmospheric pressure."

"He's vibrating, Amara. If I put a margarita shaker on his back, we'd have drinks in thirty seconds."

Dung-chul stopped pacing. He looked at Darius. He let out a long, high-pitched whine that sounded like a tea kettle dying, then walked over and wedged himself forcibly between the sofa and the coffee table, effectively barricading himself in a fortress of furniture.

"Great," Darius sighed. "Now the dog is in a bunker. We're officially under siege."

The Logistics of Dignity

The first night was defined by the humiliating mechanics of biology, but underneath that, there was a quiet, terrifying intimacy.

After a dinner of cold beef jerky and red wine (the power had flashed off right as Darius tried to boil pasta), the adrenaline of the "rescue" evaporated. It left behind two strangers in a room with one bathroom, very thin walls, and a silence so loud it hummed.

The cabin felt vast and yet incredibly small. Every sound—the settling of the wood, the pop of the fire, the shift of fabric—was amplified.

"I'll take the floor," Darius said, tossing a spare wool blanket onto the rug. He looked at the sofa where Amara was propped up like a broken doll, her leg elevated on a stack of *Architectural Digest* magazines.

"Don't be a martyr," Amara argued, her voice thick with fatigue. "You have a bad back. I heard your knees crack when you stood up. It sounded like a gunshot. Go to the bedroom. I'm fine here."

"I'm not being a martyr, I'm being practical," Darius said, kicking off his boots. The smell of damp leather filled the small space between them. "If I go to the bedroom, I can't hear you if you need... assistance. And I really don't want to wake up to find you crawling across the floor like the girl from *The Ring*."

"She crawls out of a TV," Amara corrected, rubbing her temples. "I would be crawling out of a sectional. It's different."

"Same energy. Demon vibes. I'm staying."

He slept in the armchair, legs stretched out on the ottoman, a duvet pulled up to his chin. Amara slept on the sofa.

It was a fitful, miserable night. The wind howled like a banshee. But it was the presence of another human being—and one very large, very scared animal—that kept them both awake.

At 3:14 AM, the power died for good. The sudden absence of the refrigerator's hum was deafening. The cabin plunged into a darkness so heavy it felt liquid.

Amara woke up. Her bladder was full. Her ankle was throbbing with a radioactive heat that pulsed in time with her heartbeat.

She looked at Darius. He was asleep, his head lolling to the side, mouth slightly open. He was snoring—a soft, exhausted rumble.

I can do this myself, she told herself. *I am a grown woman. I have birthed children. I manage a crisis unit.*

She sat up. The room spun. She gripped the armrest, the leather cool and slick under her sweating palms. She lowered her good foot to the floor.

Her foot landed on something warm, fur-covered, and solid.

YELP.

Dung-chul scrambled up from the darkness like a monster from the deep, scrabbling for purchase on the rug. Amara screamed, a short, sharp sound. The dog, in his panic, tried to jump onto the sofa *through* Amara, resulting in a chaotic tangle of limbs, fur, and heavy breathing.

"What! Who!?" Darius was up instantly. No grogginess. Just awake. A reflex born of years of being the person who fixed things when they broke.

"Dung-Chul!" Amara hissed, pushing seventy pounds of terrified Golden Retriever off her chest. "He was sleeping... on the floor... I stepped on him..."

"Are you bleeding?" Darius's voice was low, a weapon in the dark.

"No. I'm just... traumatized. And I need the bathroom."

"Jesus," Darius exhaled, the adrenaline leaving him in a rush. He rubbed his face, the sound of stubble rasping against his palm echoing in the quiet. "This animal is a liability. He's an insurgent."

Dung-chul, sensing the tension, let out a soft *wuff* and pressed his wet nose against Darius's hand in the dark, seeking reassurance.

"Don't try to charm me," Darius muttered, though Amara heard the soft pat-pat of his hand on the dog's head. "You almost took out the patient."

Darius stood up. He didn't turn on a flashlight. He walked over to her in the dark, navigating by memory.

"Grab my arm," he said.

He offered his forearm. It was warm and solid as a tree branch. Amara gripped it. Her fingers dug in, not because she wanted to, but because if she didn't, she would fall face-first into the rug.

They did the "shuffle-hop" waltz to the bathroom in the pitch black, their breathing synchronized by necessity. Dung-chul followed them closely, his nose bumping against the back of Darius's knee with every step, ensuring the entire procession was as dangerous as possible.

"Stop herding us," Darius whispered to the dog. "We aren't sheep."

When they reached the door, Darius opened it. He waited until she was inside.

"I'm leaving the door cracked," he announced.

"You absolutely are not," Amara hissed. "Crack. The. Door."

Amara left the door cracked one inch. From the hallway, she heard Darius start to hum. It wasn't a random tune. It was Coltrane. *A Love Supreme.* He hummed it loudly, off-key, a vibrating baritone designed to drown out the sound of her dignity shredding.

It was an act of mercy.

Part II: The Horror (Day Two)

The second day, the cabin fever set in.

The storm had knocked out the satellite internet. The phones were dead bricks. The world outside was a monochrome nightmare of gray fog and black trees.

But the real horror wasn't outside. It was inside.

It started with the smell.

Around noon, a pungent, earthy scent began to permeate the living room. It wasn't woodsmoke. It wasn't rain. It smelled like wet wool and anxiety.

"Dung-chul," Darius said, staring at the dog.

The dog was standing by the back door, vibrating. He looked at the door. He looked at Darius. He let out a whine that was so high-pitched it was practically ultrasonic.

"He has to go," Amara said from the couch.

"He can't go," Darius said, gesturing to the window where rain was currently falling *horizontally*. "It's a hurricane out there. If I open that door, we lose the roof."

"He's a dog, Darius. Biology doesn't care about wind velocity. Look at him. He's doing the potty dance."

Dung-chul was, in fact, doing a complex tap routine with his front paws, staring at the handle with desperate intensity.

Darius groaned. He grabbed his coat. He grabbed the leash.

"Fine. But if we blow away, tell my wife I died a hero."

He hooked the leash onto Dung-chul's collar. He unlocked the deadbolt. He cracked the door.

The wind didn't just enter; it invaded. It blew the magazines off the table. It blew Amara's hair back. It roared like a jet engine.

Dung-chul took one look at the swirling vortex of leaves and water, planted his four paws on the floorboards, and put on the brakes.

"Come on, buddy," Darius yelled over the wind, tugging the leash. "Let's go!"

Dung-chul refused. He lowered his center of gravity. He became a golden boulder. He looked at Darius with eyes that said, *Are you insane? There are monsters out there.*

"He won't go!" Darius yelled back at Amara.

"You have to encourage him!" Amara yelled back. "Be an Alpha!"

"I am being an Alpha! He's being a coward!"

Darius stepped out onto the porch, getting instantly soaked. He pulled. Dung-chul whined, clawing at the doorframe, trying to retreat back into the warmth.

"Just pee!" Darius screamed at the heavens. "Just pee, you furry neurotic disaster!"

Eventually, after a struggle that looked like a man wrestling a bear cub, Dung-chul managed a terrified, three-second squat on the edge of the porch before scrambling back inside, nearly tripping Darius in the process.

Darius slammed the door. He locked it. He leaned against it, dripping wet, chest heaving.

Dung-chul shook himself violently, spraying water over the entire entryway, then trotted over to the rug and lay down with a heavy sigh, looking deeply traumatized.

"I hate nature," Darius wheezed, wiping rainwater from his eyes. "I hate it so much."

But the levity didn't last.

Around 4:00 PM, the horror shifted from biological to structural.

A massive *CRACK* echoed outside—loud enough to be felt in the chest cavity.

The cabin shook. Dust fell from the rafters.

Amara screamed, a short, sharp sound. Dung-chul barked wildly, scrambling to his feet, sliding on the hardwood, his nails scratching frantically as he tried to find traction to run from an invisible enemy.

"Tree," Darius yelled, grabbing Amara's arm as if he could physically hold the cabin together. "That was a tree."

They waited. Silence. Then, the slow, agonizing groan of wood tearing. It sounded like a giant bone breaking.

CRASH.

Something massive hit the ground just yards from the back deck. The vibration traveled up through the floorboards, rattling the dishes in the cabinets. The entire structure groaned, settling deeply into the mud.

Darius ran to the back window. He wiped the condensation off the glass but forgot that he closed the outside shutters.

"Ideally," he said, his voice tight, "that fell away from the house."

"And realistically?" Amara asked, gripping the cushions. Her knuckles were white.

"Realistically, we just lost the view of the lake. There is a Douglas Fir currently making out with the deck railing. It missed the roof by... inches."

He turned back to her. His eyes were wide, adrenaline blowing out his pupils.

"We are officially under siege."

Amara started to laugh. It was a hysterical, bubbling sound. "Of course. Of course. Because the ankle wasn't enough. We needed property damage. We needed a near-death experience."

"It's the universe," Darius said, walking over to pour himself a shot of bourbon. His hand was shaking. "It's telling us we're not allowed to leave. We have to die here. Our skeletons will be found playing Scrabble in fifty years."

"I refuse to die in sweatpants and playing Scrabble," Amara said, taking the glass from his hand and downing it. She coughed, the burn bringing tears to her eyes. "If the roof caves in, I'm putting on lipstick."

Dung-chul, sensing the hysteria, crawled under the coffee table. He rested his chin on his paws and watched them with wide, mournful eyes. He knew the truth. The alpha dog outside was winning.

Part III: The Shift (Day Four)

By the fourth day, the violence of the storm had exhausted itself. The wind died down to a mournful whistle. The rain softened from a deluge to a steady, rhythmic drumming.

But inside, the pressure had shifted.

They had survived the horror. They had survived the boredom. They had survived the dog's neuroses. Now, they were surviving the intimacy.

They were stripped. After the multiple sponge baths and candelit conversations, Darius was ready to do something else.

Darius was setting up the turntable. It was the only piece of tech that still worked without a signal.

"I need music," he said. "The silence is too loud. I can hear you thinking."

"I'm not thinking," Amara lied. She was thinking about his hands. She was thinking about how he had carried her. She was thinking about the way he hummed in the hallway to protect her modesty.

"You are," he said. "You're thinking about the logistics of leaving. You're wondering if the road is clear."

"I have a practice to run," she defended. "I have patients."

"You have a calendar," Darius corrected. "And you're terrified to go back to it."

He dropped the needle on a record. *Duke Ellington & John Coltrane.*

The piano started—soft, cascading notes that sounded like rain. Then the saxophone entered—a low, smoky exhale.

"Jazz," Amara groaned. "Darius, please. Not the chaos music."

"It's not chaos," he said softly. "It's a conversation. Listen."

He didn't sit in the chair. He walked over to the sofa. He stood in front of her.

"Stand up," he said.

"My ankle..."

"Is fine. You walked to the kitchen for chips an hour ago. Stand up."

It wasn't a command. It was an invitation.

Amara looked up at him. The firelight flickered in his eyes. He looked tired. He looked lonely. He looked hungry.

She reached out. He pulled her up.

She leaned on him, her good foot taking the weight, her body pressed against his side for stability.

"I don't know how to dance to this," she whispered. "There's no beat."

"Don't count," Darius murmured, his voice rumbling in his chest against her ear. "Just feel. Follow me."

He moved. It was barely a movement. Just a sway. A shift of weight.

Amara followed. She had to. She was leaning on him, so where he went, she went.

They swayed in the dim light of the cabin. Coltrane played a run of notes that sounded like a question without an answer.

Darius pulled her closer. The gap between them closed. Amara felt the hardness of his chest. She smelled him—sandalwood, bourbon, rain, and *man*.

It was intoxicating. It was the smell of safety, but also the smell of danger. It was not something she was used to—

"You feel that?" Darius whispered. His breath ghosted over her temple.

"The music?"

"The ache," Darius said. "That's what he's playing. The blue note. The space between what you have and what you need."

Amara closed her eyes. She let her head fall forward, resting her forehead against the hollow of his shoulder.

"I feel it," she whispered. "God, Darius, I feel it."

"I know you do."

His hand on her waist slid up, just an inch. His fingers splayed out over her back, pressing her closer.

They turned slowly. Amara's bad foot dragged, but Darius took the weight. He was piloting her.

"Amara," he said. His voice was raw. Rough.

She lifted her head.

They were inches apart. The firelight cut his face into planes of gold and shadow.

He moved his hand from her waist to her face. His thumb grazed her cheekbone, brushing away a tear she hadn't realized had fallen. His skin was rough, calloused, but his touch was so tender it made her knees weak.

"You're not a liability," he whispered. The words were fierce. "You hear me? You are not a liability. Neither of us are liabilities."

Amara's breath hitched. "Darius..."

"You're the only real thing that's happened to me in ten years."

The air in the room vanished. The saxophone hit a low, long note that hung in the air like a suspended drop of water.

Amara didn't pull away. She leaned into his hand.

"I don't want to go back," she whispered. It was a confession. It was treason.

Darius leaned his forehead against hers. "Then don't."

He didn't kiss her yet. He just breathed with her. He let the tension stretch, let the hunger build until it was a physical pain in the center of the room.

"Darius," she whispered again. And this time, it was a beg.

He kissed her.

It wasn't a movie kiss. It was a collision. It was clumsy and desperate, tasting of bourbon and tears. It was the crash of two people who had been starving for so long they had forgotten how to eat.

His hands were everywhere—in her hair, on her waist, gripping her like she was the only solid thing in a world that was falling apart.

And for the first time after the storm, the horror was gone. The drama was gone.

There was only this. The touch. The shift. The moment the prop and the utility went offline, and the people underneath finally woke up.

"Tell me to stop," he said. It was not a dare. It was an invitation. "If this is just the storm talking. If this is you afraid to go back. If this is anything but you choosing me, right now."

Her world narrowed to the rough warmth of his hand on her skin, the intensity in his eyes, the way his breath hitched when she leaned in, closing that last inch. All the sensible answers lined up on the tip of her tongue: *we should wait, we shouldn't complicate this, we'll ruin everything.*

She swallowed them.

"This is me choosing you," she said.

Something shattered in his gaze—relief, hunger, years of held-back wanting snapping all at once.

His hand slid to the back of her neck, and he leaned in, and the first brush of his mouth against hers felt less like a kiss and more like finally exhaling after holding her breath for four days straight. The kiss wasn't careful. It was clumsy at first, too much urgency, teeth bumping, breath tangling, both of them laughing a little against each other's lips because of course even this was a mess.

Then it deepened, found a rhythm that had nothing to do with control and everything to do with recognition. Heat flared low in her body, startling in its intensity. The room, the storm, the record—all of it blurred to the edges as his fingers slid into her hair and she pulled him closer, her hands fisting in the soft cotton of his shirt.

"Amara," he breathed against her mouth, like a prayer or a warning.

She broke the kiss just enough to rest her forehead against his, both of them gasping, the music swirling around them in slow, liquid arcs.

"Don't be careful with me," she whispered. "Not tonight."

Whatever restraint he had left snapped.

He stood, bringing her with him, his hands braced at her waist as if he were afraid she might vanish if he let go. Her injured ankle protested when she put weight on it, and he immediately adjusted, cursing softly, lifting her without thinking.

The movement stole her breath: one second she was on the sofa, the next she was against him, his arms solid and sure, her fingers digging into his shoulders.

"Darius—"

"I've got you." The same words he'd used in the woods, but this time they vibrated with a different promise.

He turned toward the deeper shadows of the cabin, away from the window, away from the dying fire, away from everything that wasn't this impossible, reckless, necessary choice. The record kept playing, the saxophone pouring out a line that sounded exactly like falling and not caring about the landing.

As he carried her toward the dark, Amara let her head fall against his, eyes closing, the music and the storm and the blue note of them swelling until it was the only thing she could hear.

She did not think about London. She did not think about the morning. For once, she let the argument stay unresolved.

The Cartography of Scars

The journey to the bedroom was a negotiation between gravity, desire, and a Golden Retriever who refused to be excluded from the narrative.

Darius carried her down the short hallway, his breathing steady, his arms locked tight under her knees and back. Amara had her face buried in the crook of his neck, inhaling the complex map of him—the salt of dried sweat, the sharp tang of woodsmoke, the lingering bourbon, and underneath it all, something iron-rich and essential that just smelled like *Darius*.

She was trying to keep her head spinning from the kiss, but the practical side of her brain—the Utility—was already listing objections, cataloging her flaws like a forensic accountant. *I am forty-two. I am wearing cotton underwear I bought in a three-pack at Target because they were sensible. I haven't shaved my legs since Tuesday. My skin is loose where the babies lived. I am not a fantasy.*

Behind them, the rhythmic *click-click-click* of claws on hardwood followed, a relentless metronome of judgment.

"Darius," Amara whispered into his shoulder, her voice trembling. "The dog."

Darius didn't stop. He kicked the bedroom door open with his foot. "He's Korean. He's very respectful of boundaries."

"He's watching us," she hissed. "He looks concerned."

Darius walked to the bed—a massive, king-sized expanse of white duvet that looked like a cloud in the gloom. He lowered her down. He didn't drop her; he placed her. It was the way you put down something fragile and expensive, something you had spent a lifetime searching for and were terrified of breaking.

He straightened up, groaning slightly as his back popped. He looked down at the dog, who was sitting in the doorway, tail thumping slowly.

"Dung-chul," Darius said sternly, pointing a finger at the hallway. "Out. Go guard the perimeter. We are at Defcon 1."

The dog tilted his head, let out a long, judgmental sigh that rattled his jowls, walked into the room, circled three times on the rug in the far corner, and collapsed with a heavy thud, facing the wall.

"That," Darius muttered, turning back to her, "is the best I can do. He's a union worker. He's on break."

Amara let out a breathy laugh, but it caught in her throat and died when Darius stepped toward the bed. The humor evaporated, replaced by a thick, heavy silence. The only light came from the hallway, slicing a golden wedge across the duvet.

Darius sat on the edge of the bed. The mattress dipped under his weight. He didn't reach for her immediately. He just looked at her.

Amara felt exposed, even though she was fully clothed in his giant "Github" t-shirt and the baggy sweatpants. She felt shapeless. Hidden.

"I look like a laundry pile," she whispered, pulling the duvet up over her waist, her hands shaking. "This isn't... I'm not dressed for this."

"You look," Darius said, his voice low and rough, vibrating through the mattress, "like something I've been trying to find for a very long time."

He reached out. His hand hovered over her knee, heat radiating from his palm, then moved up. He hooked his fingers into the waistband of the sweatpants.

"May I?" he asked.

It wasn't a polite question. It was a check-in. It was him giving her the power she had lost twenty years ago. *Are we still doing this? Are you here with me?*

Amara nodded. She couldn't speak.

He peeled the sweatpants down, mindful of the Ace bandage on her ankle, treating the injury with a reverence that made her toes curl. He tossed them onto the floor. Then he reached for the hem of the t-shirt.

"Arms up," he murmured.

She lifted her arms. He pulled the shirt over her head. The cool air of the room hit her skin, followed immediately by the searing heat of his gaze.

Amara instinctively crossed her arms over her stomach. It was a reflex. The shame of being human. She had stretch marks that silvered her hips like lightning strikes. She had the softness that comes from years of putting everyone else first, of skipping the gym to drive the carpool, of eating the crusts off sandwiches because she hated waste.

Darius frowned. Not in disgust, but in confusion.

He reached out and took her wrists. His hands were large, warm, and impossibly gentle. He pulled her arms away from her body, pinning them softly to the mattress at her sides.

"Don't," he whispered, his eyes locking onto hers. "Don't hide from me. Not tonight. I want to see you."

"I'm not twenty-five, Darius," she said, her voice shaking, a tear slipping out. "I'm a map of errors. I'm scarred."

"You think I want a blank page?" He leaned over her, his eyes scanning her torso, drinking in the curve of her waist, the rise of her ribs. "I want the story. I want the history."

He lowered his head. He didn't kiss her lips. He kissed her shoulder. Then her collarbone. Then the soft swell of her breast above her bra. Then, he moved lower.

He stopped at the scar.

The C-section line was a faint, horizontal slash across her lower belly. It was the mark of emergency, of fear, of the moment she became a mother. Carter had never looked at it. He looked *past* it. He treated it like a flaw in the drywall that they just agreed to ignore.

Darius traced it with his thumb. The callus on his skin caught slightly on the smooth tissue. Amara flinched, sucking in a breath.

"It's ugly."

"It's a door," Darius murmured, his voice thick with emotion.

He pressed a kiss to the center of the scar, his lips hot against the cool skin.

Amara gasped. Her back arched off the mattress. A shockwave went through her, shattering the shame.

"It's the way life got into the room," Darius whispered against her skin. "How is that ugly? It's a miracle."

He kissed it again. And again. Worshiping the trauma. Reclaiming the ground.

Amara stared at the ceiling, tears streaming freely now. She had spent twenty years hearing the myth of the Black man in America—the aggressor, the danger. But this? This was the truth she had known in her bones but had forgotten. There are no hands as gentle as a Black man's hands when he loves something. There is no reverence like the reverence of a man who knows what it costs to survive in a body that the world wants to break.

"Darius," she choked out, her hands finding his hair, pulling him closer.

He found the clasp of her bra. *Snap.* The restriction fell away. He hovered over her, supporting his weight on his elbows so he wouldn't crush her.

"You are spectacular," he said. And he looked shocked by it. Like he had stumbled onto a shoreline he didn't know existed. "Amara. Look at you."

"I'm looking at you," she whispered. She reached up and touched his face. She traced the gray in his beard, the exhaustion lines around his eyes. "You're beautiful, Darius."

He let out a ragged breath, closing his eyes against her palm. "I'm just a prop."

"No," she said fiercely, pulling his face down to hers. "You're the lead. You are the whole damn show."

When he kissed her this time, it wasn't the clumsy collision of the living room. It was a slow, deep drowning.

His hands were everywhere. They were rough, yes, but they moved with a terrifying precision. He found the spot behind her ear that made her shiver. He found the curve of her spine that made her melt. He made her realize that for twenty years, she had been touched in black and white. Darius was touching her in color.

They moved together in the dark, bathed in the sound of the rain and the heavy, rhythmic breathing of two people breaking a fast. It was messy. It was human. It was sweat and friction and the desperate need to be inside someone else's skin because your own was too lonely.

At one point, Dung-chul let out a loud, yipping bark in his sleep, causing them both to freeze, hearts pounding, before dissolving into breathless, sweaty giggles against each other's necks.

"He's dreaming of squirrels," Darius whispered into her hair, his chest shaking with laughter.

"He's critiquing your form," Amara whispered back, biting his shoulder.

"My form is impeccable," Darius growled, and then he moved, and the laughter turned into a gasp, and the world narrowed down to heat and *finally, finally* being found.

CHAPTER 5: THE SANCTUARY

Morning came too fast. It arrived with a brilliant, blinding streak of sunlight that cut through the shutters, announcing that the storm was over.

The world was back.

They lay in bed for a long time, not speaking. The room smelled of sex and sleep. Darius was on his back, arm thrown over his eyes to block the sun. Amara was resting on his chest, tracing the line of his tattoo—a geometric pattern on his bicep. Interestingly enough, neither felt a piece of guilt.

"The road will be clear," Darius said. His voice was flat.

"Yes," Amara said. She didn't move. She couldn't bear to break the contact.

"We have to go back."

"I know."

Darius moved his arm. He turned to look at her. His eyes were clear, serious, devoid of the morning-after regret she feared. He didn't look like a man who had made a mistake. He looked like a man who had made a discovery.

"I'm not losing you, Amara," he said. "I don't care how complicated the math is. I am not going back to being a ghost."

Amara sat up, pulling the sheet around her. The reality of the day crashed into the room. "We can't text," she said, her therapist brain engaging, the Utility trying to protect the Prop. "Sasha checks your phone?"

"She checks the cloud," Darius said, sitting up. "She syncs everything. Her insecurity is digitized. She treats my location data like a soothing ritual."

"And Carter?"

"He doesn't check," Amara said dryly. "He assumes I'm boring. He assumes I'm incapable of deception because deception requires too much administrative overhead. But the kids... they use my iPad. They track me."

Darius nodded. He reached for his jeans on the floor. Amara watched him, expecting him to pull out his wallet or his keys. Instead, he pulled a small, silver thumb drive from the pocket.

He held it out like it was a ring.

"ProtonMail," he said.

Amara frowned. "What?"

"It's an encrypted email service based in Switzerland. I use it for IP transfers. I'm going to set up an account for you right now. No app on the phone. Browser only. Incognito mode."

He handed her the drive.

"We write drafts," he said. "We don't send emails. We just save them in the drafts folder. If anyone hacks it, the inbox is empty. It's a dead drop."

Amara took the drive. It felt heavy. It felt like a weapon. It felt like a promise.

"Drafts," she repeated.

"Drafts," Darius confirmed. He leaned in and kissed her forehead. It was a chaste kiss, reverent and sad, sealing the pact. "We log in. We write. We save. We never send."

He stood up and walked to the window, opening the shutter he had kept closed for four days. The light flooded the room, illuminating the dust motes, the tangled sheets, the clothes scattered on the floor. In that moment, the power returns.

"Yes! Now get dressed," he said, looking back at her with a fierce, possessive tenderness. "Before I decide to barricade the door and keep you here forever."

Amara clutched the silver drive in her hand. The storm was over, but the rebellion had just begun.

Amara clutched the silver drive in her hand. The storm was over, but the rebellion had just begun. She moved her ankle—it was tight but didnt hurt really bad.

And then, with a jarring, cheerful *beep* that sounded like a mockingbird, the microwave clock flashed **12:00**.

The sound was followed immediately by the refrigerator humming to life—a heavy, mechanical shudder like a beast waking from hibernation. In the bathroom, the exhaust fan kicked on with a rattle, sucking the steam and the silence out of the air.

The cabin, which had been a womb for seventy-two hours, suddenly felt like an appliance store.

"And just like that," Darius sighed, watching the digital numbers blink. "The acoustic set is over. Welcome back to the grid."

He didn't immediately move to get dressed. Instead, he walked to the kitchen island, his bare feet padding softly on the cold heart-pine floors. He looked at the automatic coffee maker, which had been sitting dormant and useless for three days. It began to gurgle aggressively, spitting steam, eager to perform its only function.

"Do you hear that?" Darius asked, gesturing to the machine. "That is the sound of efficiency. It's disgusting."

"It's aggressive," Amara agreed, using the walls to approach him. She had on a duvet from the bed, wrapped around her shoulders like a heavy, down-filled cape. She climbed onto one of the barstools, pulling her knees to her chest. She wasn't ready to be a person yet. She was still a raw nerve ending.

"Do you want the last of the powdered milk?" Darius asked, peering into a ceramic canister with the skepticism of a bomb squad technician. "Or should we celebrate our return to civilization with black coffee and existential dread? I need to clean a bit."

"Black," Amara said. "I need the bitterness. It'll help me transition. What can I do?"

"You can sit there."

Darius poured two mugs. The steam rose in the cold morning air, smelling of roasted beans and inevitability. He slid one across the granite counter to her.

"So," he said, leaning his hip against the island, wrapping his large hands around the mug. "Brief me. We have maybe an hour before we have to clear the blast radius. What exactly are you walking into? If I have to go back to being a Prop, I need to know the Utility is suffering just as much."

Amara blew on her coffee. She looked out the window where the sun was brutally, cheerfully melting the dreary.

"You want the report?" she asked.

"I want the autopsy."

"Okay." Amara took a sip. "I will walk through the door. The house will smell like essential oils—probably lemongrass, because Carter read an article that said lemongrass promotes 'cognitive fluidity.' He will be sitting at the dining room table. He will be surrounded by three different laptops and a stack of books on post-colonial agrarian reform."

"Sounds intellectual," Darius said dryly.

"It's performance art," Amara countered. "He will look up. He won't ask if I'm okay. He won't ask if I survived the storm. He will look at me with these soulful, tragic eyes and say, 'Amara, the router is blinking orange. Does this signify a structural collapse of the telecommunications infrastructure, or do I need to unplug it?'"

Darius laughed—a low, rumbling sound that vibrated in his chest.

"He can't fix the router?"

"Darius, the man has a PhD. He can deconstruct the Hegelian dialectic in his sleep. But if the WiFi goes down? He becomes a toddler. A bearded, tenure-track toddler. He believes that 'technical support' is a form of oppression. He thinks the router should just *know* he needs to upload his syllabus."

"Weaponized incompetence," Darius diagnosed, nodding. "Classic."

"It's not just incompetence," Amara said, her voice rising with the heat of the memory. "It's the *narrative* of incompetence. If he washes a dish, he needs a parade. If he drives the kids to soccer, he treats it like a sociological field study. 'Amara,' he'll say, 'the tribalism of suburban sports is fascinating.' And I'm like, 'Carter, did you remember the Gatorade?' and he looks at me like I'm speaking capitalism."

She groaned, dropping her forehead onto her knees. "I am the Chief Logistics Officer of a non-profit that doesn't actually help anyone. I keep the lights on so he can write papers about how electricity is a social construct."

Darius took a long swallow of coffee. His eyes were dark, amused, but filled with a mirror-image fatigue.

"I envy the chaos," he said. "At least your house has dirt. At least it has friction."

"And yours?"

"My house is a museum," Darius said. "A museum dedicated to the concept of 'Everything is Fine.' My pain has a color scheme, Amara. It's usually 'Greige' or 'Coastal Calm.'"

He set the mug down. "I will walk in. Sasha will be in the 'staging area'—formerly known as our living room. She will have set up a ring light and a tripod. She won't say, 'Hello, husband, I'm glad you didn't die in the woods.' She will say, 'Babe, don't move. I mean, I would have to tell her first. The lighting is hitting your cheekbones perfectly. Grab the Goldendoodle and look pensive near the window. We need to capture *Sunday Serenity* for the followers."

"She scripts the greeting?" Amara asked, horrified.

"She scripts the *atmosphere*," Darius corrected. "If I look tired, she filters it to make me look 'rugged.' If I look angry, she captions it 'Intense focus.' I am not a husband, Amara. I am content. I am a prop in a reality show that airs exclusively on her iPhone to an audience of women she hates from her sorority days."

He ran a hand over his face. "And the worst part? She's terrified. If there is a moment of silence—real silence, not curated silence—she panics. She thinks if she stops posting, she disappears. So I have to be the audience. I have to clap. I have to validate the performance. 'Yes, honey, the organic kale chips look beautiful.' 'Yes, the monochromatic Christmas tree is very chic,' even though it looks like a depression ward."

Amara watched him. She saw the exhaustion in the slope of his shoulders. It wasn't the exhaustion of work; it was the exhaustion of being erased.

"And the shareholders?" she asked softly. "The kids?"

Darius's face shifted. A complicated mix of pride and terror took over.

"The twins, Mike and Bea. They are sixteen going on assholes."

"The economists."

"The Venture Capitalists," Darius corrected. "They don't want a hug or advice. Last week, I tried to do something with them, and they called me corny. They looked at me and asked whether we could discuss his custodial Roth IRA, since they want a new car. They think it's that easy to buy a car."

Amara choked on her coffee. "They are sixteen?"

"They track the S&P 500. Like their mom, they care more about spending than about actually earning it. I have to negotiate with them, Amara. I wanted better for my kids, but this ain't it. I have to have a quarterly earnings call with kids. They look at me with this disappointment, like, 'Father, your ROI on family finances is suboptimal.' They are going to put me in a home the second I stop being profitable."

"That's terrifying," Amara whispered.

"It's effective," Darius said. "They'll rule the world because they're greedy like the buttholes running the world now. But I miss... I don't know. I miss a kid who just wants to ride a bike. Who scrapes his or her knee."

"I have the opposite problem," Amara said. "Keela. Sixteen."

"The activist?"

"The Prosecutor," Amara said. "She currently hates me. Not because I'm mean, but because I am a 'tool of the patriarchy' for asking her to empty the dishwasher. She stands there, Darius, holding a dirty plate, and gives me a lecture on how domestic labor is the unpaid spine of capitalism. She uses words like 'heteronormative conditioning' while I am literally scrubbing her crusty oatmeal out of a bowl."

"Smart girl," Darius noted.

"Too smart," Amara said. "She cancels me three times a week. I bought the wrong almond milk? I'm supporting a drought in California. I bought her new jeans? I'm contributing to fast-fashion landfills. But then—and this is the kicker—she asks me for twenty dollars to go to the mall to buy 'vintage' jeans that look exactly like the ones I threw away in 1998. She hates the system, but she needs a ride to the protest in the Volvo."

They sat in silence for a moment, the hum of the refrigerator filling the space. It was a comfortable silence. A truthful one. They weren't complaining to be mean; they were complaining to survive. They were acknowledging the absurdity of the lives they had built— the expensive, polished, heavy cages.

"And Marcus, right?" Darius asked gently. "The younger one?"

Amara smiled, but it was a tired smile. "Marcus is... Marcus is a terrorist. A terrorist."

"Picky?"

"Darius, the child only eats beige food. Nuggets. Fries. Crackers. Bread. If a vegetable touches his plate, he screams like I've presented him with a radioactive isotope. I spend three hours a night negotiating with a twelve-year-old. — loud, dramatic, and permanently confused about why the world didn't operate on *his* internal schedule. He had the emotional range of a malfunctioning smart speaker: either completely silent or screaming because someone finished the cereal he wasn't planning to eat. He communicated exclusively in complaints, snack requests, and the phrase "Why is there no milk," as if Amara personally drank it out of spite. He was too old to be this helpless and too young to be this opinionated. A walking contradiction in mismatched socks. A boy who could operate three gaming systems at once but somehow could not locate a gallon of milk sitting directly in front of him in the refrigerator.

Marcus was her baby — her last nerve and her soft spot — a tiny, hormonal tornado who treated every minor inconvenience like a federal emergency and every chore like a human rights violation.

She looked down at her hands. "I love them," she whispered. "God, I love them so much it hurts. But I am so tired of managing them. I'm tired of being the buffer between them and reality."

"We are middle management," Darius said softly. He walked around the island and stood between her knees. "That's what we are. We aren't partners. We aren't parents. We are the Chief Operations Officers of their delusions."

"We are the fixers," Amara agreed, leaning forward until her forehead rested against his bare stomach. His skin was warm. Real. "I fix Carter's incompetence. You fix Sasha's insecurity. You fix Little D's portfolio. I fix Keela's moral outrage. Who fixes us?"

Darius placed his hands on her head, stroking her hair. The intimacy of it was shocking in the bright kitchen light.

"We do," he said. "That's what ProtonMail is for. That's what the drafts are. It's the break room. It's the only place we don't have to be efficient."

"I don't want to go back," Amara mumbled into his skin. "I don't want to go back to being a 'Tool of the Patriarchy.' I want to stay here and drink bad coffee and listen to you complain about your kid's stock portfolio."

"We have to go," Darius said. "Because if we don't go back, the machinery breaks. And if the machinery breaks, they come looking for us."

He pulled away slightly, checking the watch on his wrist.

"However," he said, a slow, wicked grin spreading across his face. It was the smile of a man who knew how to cook the books.

"What?"

"If we leave right now, we beat the traffic. We get back to Atlanta in two hours. I'm home by 2:30."

"Okay..."

"But," Darius continued, "if we stay here... if we have another cup of coffee... maybe take a shower... we hit the Sunday afternoon gridlock on the 400. It's brutal. Bumper to bumper. A complete standstill."

Amara looked at him. She began to smile.

"Which means," Darius said, "I would have a legitimate, verifiable excuse for being late. 'Sorry, babe. Nightmare traffic. A tractor-trailer jackknifed. Couldn't make the photo shoot. I'm devastated.'"

"And Carter," Amara added, the gears turning, "doesn't check traffic apps. He thinks Waze is surveillance capitalism. I could tell him the road out of the mountains was still blocked by a tree. He'd believe it. He'd probably write a poem about the tree."

"Forty-five minutes," Darius said. "Maybe an hour. Of pure, unadulterated inefficiency."

"We should probably use that time to clean the cabin," Amara said, not moving.

"We should," Darius agreed, not moving. "We should definitely sweep the floor."

"And strip the bed."

"Absolutely. Stripping the bed is a priority."

Darius reached out and took the coffee mug from her hands. He set it on the counter. Then he put his hands on her waist and lifted her off the stool. The duvet fell to the floor, a puddle of feathers and cotton.

"Let's go be inefficient," he whispered.

"Terribly," Amara agreed.

And for the next hour, nobody managed anything at all.

CHAPTER 6: THE RE-ENTRY
(THE BENDS)

Part I: The Air-Conditioned Nightmare

Darius didn't drive his SUV home.

The road crews had cleared the fallen hemlock from the driveway of Cabin Two, dragging the heavy, wet wood aside like a dead body, but Darius couldn't bring himself to get behind the wheel. The act of driving felt too active, too engaged. He wasn't ready to participate in traffic. He wasn't ready to participate in America.

He left the Expedition in the garage at the rental office on the peninsula, handed the keys to a confused teenager with braces, and booked an Uber for the three-hour ride to SeaTac, followed by a red-eye to Atlanta.

He needed to be cargo.

The flight was a blur of compressed air and pretzel packets. He landed in Atlanta at 3:30 PM on a Tuesday. The humidity hit him the moment the automatic doors slid open at Hartsfield-Jackson—a wet, hot towel slapped across his face. It smelled of jet fuel, asphalt, and the distinct, sugary rot of the South.

He summoned another Uber. A Toyota Camry this time, smelling aggressively of "Black Ice" air freshener and stale filtered cigarettes.

The ride to Buckhead was a slow-motion trauma.

For four days, Darius's visual diet had been restricted to bland water, green firs, and the warm, amber light of a fireplace. Now, the world was screaming at him. Billboards for personal injury lawyers (*In a Wreck? Get a Check!*) fought for space with digital signs flashing wait times for the ER. The highway was a river of red brake lights.

Honk. Honk. Swerve.

He felt a physical pressure behind his eyes, a throbbing headache that wasn't from dehydration, but from processing speed. He was a dial-up modem trying to download a 5G world. He had the bends.

The Uber driver, a man named Kevin who was listening to a podcast about crypto-currency at full volume, glanced in the rearview mirror.

"You look like you been through it, boss," Kevin said. "Business or pleasure?"

Darius looked out the window at the concrete retaining wall of I-85. "Rescue mission," he said.

"Yeah? You save the girl?"

Darius thought about Amara's ankle. He thought about the C-section scar under his thumb. He thought about the silver thumb drive burning a hole in his pocket.

"I think," Darius said quietly, "she saved me."

Kevin nodded sagely. "That's beautiful, man. Bitcoin is kinda saving me right now, too."

When the car finally pulled up to the house in Buckhead, the neighborhood's silence felt artificial. It wasn't the heavy, living silence of the Olympic Peninsula. It was the manicured silence of money.

The lawn was cut to within a millimeter of its life, a carpet of unnatural green. The hedges were boxed into submission. The white brick of the colonial facade gleamed in the afternoon sun, looking less like a home and more like a set piece for a movie about people who smile too much.

It looked perfect. It looked dead.

Darius got out. He didn't walk to the front door. The front door opened into the grand foyer, a two-story echo chamber of marble and mirrors where Sasha liked to stage her "Welcome" shots. He wasn't ready for the stage.

He walked around the side of the house, his boots crushing the perfectly mulched azalea beds. He went straight to the heavy, reinforced steel door that led to the basement.

He punched in the code on the digital keypad. *9-4-1-7.*

Click. Whir. Thunk.

The door swung open.

The smell hit him first—or rather, the lack of it. The air down here was filtered, cool, and aggressively neutral. This wasn't a storage room. This was a fully finished, 1,200-square-foot sanctuary that the rest of the family treated like a forbidden zone.

It had a full kitchenette with a slate backsplash, a bathroom with a steam shower, and a wall of servers where he kept his life's work encrypted. The blue LEDs of the server rack blinked in the darkness —a rhythmic, binary heartbeat.

Sasha hated it down here. She called it "The Cave." She claimed the WiFi signal died down here (it didn't; Darius had hardwired it specifically to be faster than the rest of the house). She avoided it because she couldn't control the lighting, and the acoustics were "too dead" for her videos.

Darius stepped inside and threw the deadbolt.

Thunk.

He was home. But he wasn't *back*.

He dropped his duffel bag on the polished concrete floor. He didn't unpack his clothes. He unpacked the turntable. He set it up on the credenza next to his monitors. He took out the Coltrane record, sliding it from the sleeve with the same reverence he had used in the cabin.

He poured a drink from the wet bar—not the performative Pappy Van Winkle he served upstairs, but a solid, high-proof rye he kept for late nights coding.

He spent the night underground.

He could hear them upstairs. The muffled *thump-thump* of the twins running down the hall. The *click-clack* of Sasha's heels on the hardwood. The distant, tiny sound of a television. But they felt miles away. They were noises from the surface; he was deep-sea.

He showered in the steam shower, washing the smell of the cabin off his skin—the pine, the rain, the smoke. But as the water hit his chest, he realized he couldn't scrub away the phantom sensation of Amara's hand resting there.

He ate a protein bar from his emergency stash. He slept in the leather armchair, wrapped in a blanket, staring at the blinking lights of his server rack.

He was calibrating.

Part II: The Content House

At 8:00 AM the next morning, Darius realized he needed real coffee.

The basement kitchenette had only emergency rations and freeze-dried espresso powder, and he refused to drink the pod coffee upstairs, which tasted like burnt plastic and convenience. He needed the bean-to-cup machine in the main kitchen.

He grabbed his keys. He didn't go up the main internal stairs. He exited through the side door that connected the basement directly to the garage.

He opened the door and stepped onto the concrete floor of the three-car garage.

The air smelled of tire rubber and expensive detailing spray. And standing there, bathed in the harsh, fluorescent overhead lights, was Sasha.

She was standing by her white Range Rover, dressed in a matching beige athleisure set that looked like it cost more than his first car. She was holding a green juice in one hand—the condensation dripping onto her manicure—and her phone in the other.

She was recording.

"...so today is about *intention*, guys," she was saying to the screen, her voice pitched up into that breathless, motivational register that made Darius's teeth ache. "We are manifesting abundance and clearing the energy for the weekend. I woke up feeling so—"

She stopped. She saw him.

Darius stood there in his wrinkled jeans and the hoodie he had worn for three days. He looked unshaven. He looked like a man who had just emerged from a bunker after the apocalypse, blinking in the nuclear winter.

"Darius?" she gasped, lowering the phone. "Oh my god! When did you get back? The garage was empty last night!"

"I took an Uber," Darius said, his voice rusty. He walked past her toward the third bay, where his vintage Porsche 911 sat under a dust cover. "I got in late. I slept downstairs."

Sasha blinked. Her brain buffered for a second, processing the information. *Uber. Downstairs. Late.* Then, the instinct kicked in. The Brand took over.

"Wait!" She pulled the phone back up, swiping frantically to the camera app.

"Babe, wait! Don't get in the car yet! This is perfect! The lighting is actually really good right here. Let's do a 'Surprise Return' reel. Just walk through the door again—go back in—and come out looking tired but happy! Like, 'Honey, I'm home!' energy."

She positioned herself, holding the phone up, the ring light case casting a harsh halo in the dim garage. She tapped the screen to lock focus.

"Okay, ready?" she chirped, putting on her camera smile—a dazzling, terrifying display of teeth. "And... action! Look who's finally home!"

Darius stopped with his hand on the door handle of the Porsche.

He looked at the phone lens. It was a black, unblinking eye.

He looked at his wife. She wasn't looking at him. She was looking at the *image* of him on her screen. She was checking the framing. She was checking the filter. She was editing him in real-time.

For twenty years, he had smiled. He had waved. He had been the dutiful, successful husband who validated her narrative of the perfect life. He had been the Prop.

But the Prop had stayed in the woods.

"No," he said calmly.

The word hung in the garage, heavy and solid.

"What?" Sasha lowered the phone slightly, her smile faltering.

"No reel, Sasha."

He yanked the cover off the Porsche. It slid to the floor in a pool of silver fabric. He opened the car door.

"But people have been asking where you are!" she protested, stepping closer, the phone still recording. "It's good content, D! Just give me a wave! Just say hi to the squad!"

Darius slid into the driver's seat. The leather was cold. It smelled of oil and old horsehair—a real smell. He keyed the ignition.

The engine roared to life—a raw, mechanical bark that echoed off the concrete walls, drowning out her voice.

He didn't wave. He didn't look back. He hit the garage door opener and backed out into the morning sun, leaving her standing there, a beige statue holding a glowing rectangle, filming a car driving away from her life.

Part III: The Noise

Three thousand miles away, Amara Lewis pulled into her driveway in Portland just as the sun was setting.

The house was a craftsman bungalow that needed painting. The front yard was a battlefield. Two bikes were thrown across the lawn like casualties of war. The recycling bin had been knocked over by the wind, spilling soda cans and cardboard Amazon boxes across the driveway in a wet, soggy trail.

Usually, this sight made her chest tighten. Usually, the Utility would rush to pick up the bin before even going inside, fixing the facade before tending to herself. She would apologize to the neighbors in her head. She would catalog the failure.

Today, she stepped over the recycling.

She walked through the front door. The sensory assault was immediate.

The house smelled of stale pepperoni pizza, unwashed gym socks, and damp dog, even though Dung-Chul was with her. It was the smell of a fraternity house run by teenagers.

"Mom?" Keela's voice came from the living room. "Where have you been? Dad said you were lost in the woods or something. There's no milk."

Amara walked into the living room.

Keela was sprawled on the couch, illuminated by the blue light of her phone. Marcus, her youngest, was playing a video game, headset on, screaming, *"He's flanking! He's flanking!"* at a screen.

Carter was at the dining table, surrounded by piles of construction invoices. He looked up, his glasses sliding down his nose.

They all looked at her.

They expected the apology. They expected the flurry of activity —the grocery run, the laundry starting, the soothing *"I'm sorry I worried you, let me fix everything."* They expected the machine to turn back on.

Amara stood in the center of the room. She was still wearing the "Github" t-shirt tucked into her jeans. Her braids were messy, windblown from the drive. She wasn't wearing makeup.

And she was glowing.

There was a flush to her skin that hadn't been there in years. Her shoulders were back. She looked full. She looked like a woman who had a secret that was keeping her warm.

"Hi," Amara said. Her voice was calm, distinct. It cut through the noise of the video game.

"There's no milk," Keela repeated, uncertainly. She sensed the shift. The WiFi signal was different. It wasn't serving; it was broadcasting.

"Then drink water," Amara said pleasantly.

She walked past them. She walked past the kitchen, where the sink was piled high with three days of dishes. She walked to the narrow staircase that led to the unfinished attic.

"Amara?" Carter stood up. He looked confused. He walked over to her, intercepting her at the bottom of the stairs.

"Where are you going? I thought we'd order Thai. You've been gone a week. I missed you."

He reached out and grabbed her waist.

It was a familiar, proprietary grab. A husband claiming his wife. His hands were heavy, familiar, and utterly devoid of question.

"I missed you," he repeated, his voice dropping to that specific tone that meant *I want sex because it's Tuesday and I'm stressed.*

Amara flinched.

His hands felt wrong. They felt light. They felt unaware. They felt like strangers' hands compared to the heavy, reverent weight of Darius. Darius had touched her like he was reading braille; Carter was touching her like he was checking for his wallet.

She stepped back, removing his hands from her waist firmly.

"Not tonight, Carter," she said.

She didn't apologize. She didn't make an excuse about a headache. She just said no.

"But—"

"I'm tired," she said. She smiled. It was a secret smile, one that had nothing to do with him. "I'm going to the attic."

"The attic? It's full of dust. It's freezing up there. What are you going to do?"

"I know," Amara said. "I'm going to clear it out. I need a room. A room that is just mine."

She turned and walked up the stairs, the wood creaking under her boots. She left her husband and children staring after her, shocked into silence.

Part IV: The Digital Pact

Inside the dusty attic, Amara pushed a box of old toys aside.

The air was cold and smelled of insulation and old cedar. Dust motes danced in the light of the streetlamp filtering through the single dormer window. It wasn't the cabin, but it was quiet.

She cleared a small circle on the floorboards. She sat down, crossing her legs. She closed her eyes.

She pulled the memory of Cabin Two around her like a blanket. She could smell the sandalwood. She could feel the weight of Darius's hand on her belly. She could hear the saxophone's blue note.

She took a deep breath, filling her lungs with the dust and the memory, and for the first time in twenty years, she didn't feel lonely in her own house.

She pulled the silver thumb drive from her pocket. She plugged it into her iPad using the adapter Darius had given her.

She opened the browser. *Incognito Mode.*

ProtonMail.com.

She typed in the username he had written on the slip of paper: UnionLocal303.

She typed the password: BlueNote1964.

The inbox was empty. Just as he promised. A dead drop.

She clicked on **Drafts**.

The number next to the folder changed.

Her heart hammered against her ribs. She clicked it.

Subject: The Bends

Saved: Today, 8:42 PM

The house is loud. The lights are too bright. I tried to drink the coffee here and it tastes like plastic. Sasha tried to film me in the garage. I walked away. I'm in the basement now. The server lights are blue, but they aren't the lake.

I miss the rain. I miss the tea. I miss the way you listen.

Tell me you're there. Tell me I didn't imagine it.

Amara let out a sob—just one, sharp and sudden. She pressed her hand to her mouth. She wasn't crazy. He was real. The peace was real.

She hit **Reply**. She didn't type a salutation.

I'm here. I'm listening. My house smells like gym socks and my husband wants to pretend I never left. I'm in the attic. It's cold, but I'm still warm. They clearly showed my that I am the maid.

You didn't imagine it. We are the only real things.

She hit **Save**.

The draft count went to.

Downstairs, the TV blared. Carter dropped a plate. Keela shouted for her cleats. The noise of the Utility's life rushed against the floorboards.

But in the attic, in the glow of the screen, Amara sat in the silence of the Union. And for the first time, she didn't rush down to fix the noise. She let it ring.

CHAPTER 7: THE DIGITAL LIFELINE (THE GHOST NETWORK)

The affair didn't happen in a hotel room. It didn't happen with stolen touches in an elevator or hushed phone calls from a car idling in a driveway.

It happened in the terrifying, electrified silence of the **Drafts** folder.

They didn't sext. Sexting was for people who wanted friction, for people who wanted to perform desire. Darius and Amara wanted oxygen. They used ProtonMail for the long letters—the soulful, midnight confessions typed out on glowing screens in the Attic and the Fortress.

But they never hit "Send."

Sending created a paper trail. Sending created a notification. Sending meant the data traveled across servers that could be subpoenaed, intercepted, or synced to a family cloud.

Instead, they logged into a shared account—*UnionLocal303*—typed their souls into a blank email, and hit **Save**.

It was a ghost town, with only two people living there. A digital room where they could leave notes on the refrigerator door, knowing the other would find them.

For the day-to-day triage, for the moments when they felt their old lives closing in like a trash compactor, Darius had installed a hidden app on Amara's iPad and phone called **Calculator+**.

To Carter, if he ever looked (which he didn't, because the logistics of their life were "Amara's domain"), it looked like a budgeting tool. To Sasha, who tracked apps like a hawk, it looked like utility.

To Amara and Darius, it was a lifeline. It was a constant, invisible hum in their pockets. A ghost network that ran beneath the surface of their real lives, keeping the signal alive.

Part I: The ATM Glitch

Tuesday Morning. Atlanta.

The kitchen was a masterpiece of cold marble and stainless steel, illuminated by under-cabinet lighting that made the room feel like an operating theater. Darius stood at the espresso machine, watching the dark liquid drip into his cup.

He was wearing his "costume"—a crisp, charcoal button-down and tailored slacks. He hated this shirt. It felt stiff, starching his posture into something rigid and yielding. It felt like wearing a straitjacket made of Egyptian cotton.

The air pressure in the kitchen changed.

The twins, Mike and Bea, materialized. They didn't walk in; they seemed to spawn near the sub-zero refrigerator, absorbing the light around them.

They were sixteen, beautiful, and terrifyingly indifferent. They moved with the confident lethargy of people who had never worried about a utility bill in their lives.

"Dad," Mike said. He didn't look up from his phone. "I need three hundred."

"School trip deposit," Bea added, examining her acrylic nails, which were painted a shade of 'blood red' that Darius found vaguely threatening. "Due today. Mom said ask you."

In the old timeline—the timeline before the cabin, before the music, before the scar—Darius would have sighed. He would have felt the familiar crush of being a resource rather than a person. He would have pulled out his phone, opened Venmo, and paid the "Portal Tax" just to make them go away.

But today, his phone buzzed against his thigh. *Calculator+*.

He slipped his hand into his pocket. The phone was warm, a small brick of heat against his leg. He thumbed the code without looking.

Darius: *Extraction team is here. Asking for $300. I'm reaching for the wallet. It's a reflex. I feel sick.*

The response was instant.

Amara: *Stop. Close the wallet. You are not an ATM. Interview them. If they don't look at you, they don't get paid. Breathe, Darius.*

Darius stared at the counter. *Breathe.*

He put the phone face down. He picked up his espresso. He turned to his children.

"No," Darius said.

The silence that followed was absolute. It was the silence of a glitch. Mike stopped scrolling. Bea's mouth fell open. It was the look of someone pushing a button on a vending machine and getting nothing back but a mechanical whir.

"What?" Mike asked, his tone annoyed, bordering on offended. "Dad, it's due today."

"I said no," Darius said, taking a sip. The coffee was bitter. It grounded him. "Not until you tell me what the topic is. Specifically. Sell me on the investment. Since ya'll always wanna be in my pockets, convince me."

The twins exchanged a panicked look. They didn't have a script for this. The NPC (Non-Player Character) had gone rogue. The NPC was asking questions.

"It's... a field trip," Mike stammered. "To the Capitol."

"For what purpose?" Darius asked. "Are you lobbying? Are you protesting? Are you eating Chick-fil-A in the food court? If you want three hundred dollars of my labor, you need to explain why it's worth it."

"Dad, we're going to be late," Bea whined, opting for the strategy that usually worked: urgency. "Just send it. Mom would just send it."

"Then ask your mother," Darius said calmly. "But the Bank of Dad is currently under audit. It is closed for renovations. I have too much money going out and no return."

Mike stared at him. He realized the portal was locked. His brain engaged. He actually looked at his father—not at the wallet, but at the face.

"It's... agricultural subsidies," Mike said, pulling the words from a hazy memory of a syllabus.

"Fascinating," Darius said. He leaned back against the counter, crossing his arms. "Argue the affirmative. Give me one point. Why should we subsidize corn?"

"Uh..." Mike blinked. "Because... without subsidies, small farms can't compete with global markets? It leads to... food insecurity?"

It was a C-minus argument. It was barely a sentence. But it was an effort. It was a synapse firing.

Darius nodded slowly. He picked up his phone. He sent the Venmo.

"Food security," Darius said. "Valid point. The transaction is approved nut only for $50.00."

"$50.00 measely dollars, Bea screamed." Mike snatched Bea by the arm and said, "We'll take it!"

He hit send.

"Have a good day," he said.

The twins took the money and fled, grabbed their backpacks, and rushed out the door, looking back at him with a mixture of confusion. They looked like they had just encountered a bear in the kitchen.

Darius leaned against the counter, his hands shaking from the adrenaline. He opened the app.

Darius: *I made him debate corn subsidies. He looked terrified. But he did it. He looked me in the eye.*

Amara: *10 points to Gryffindor. See? You exist.*

Part II: The Utility Outage

Wednesday Evening. Portland.

The kitchen smelled of stale pizza crusts, wet dog, and the sharp, metallic scent of anxiety.

Amara was at the island, chopping bell peppers with violent precision. *Thwack. Thwack. Thwack.*

She had spent ten hours listening to patients. She had absorbed the grief of a widow, the panic of a grad student, and the rage of a divorcee. She was full. She was overflowing.

She had come home to find the sink full of dishes again, the recycling bin overflowing, and Carter standing in the doorway holding a glass of wine he hadn't offered to share.

"The dry cleaning, Amara?" Carter asked, checking his phone. "I have a presentation tomorrow for a client. I put the blue suit on the calendar. I put a reminder on your phone."

"I didn't go," Amara said, chopping harder. "Crisis patient. Suicidal ideation. I couldn't leave."

"I understand," Carter sighed, the sound heavy with martyrdom. "But logistics are your thing, Amara. I rely on you. I need the suit. Now I have to wear the gray one, and the gray one pulls at the shoulders."

Keela walked in, wearing vintage clothes Amara had paid for—an oversized flannel and jeans that cost more than Amara's entire wardrobe. She dropped her backpack on the floor, right where Amara would have to step over it.

"Mom, are you making stir-fry?" Keela asked, wrinkling her nose. "I told you, nightshades cause inflammation. You're poisoning the vibe."

"Then pick them out," Amara snapped, the knife hitting the cutting board with a loud *crack*.

"God, you're so aggressive lately," Keela scoffed, rolling her eyes. "It's like walking on eggshells. You used to be chill."

The Utility light flickered. Amara felt the crush of erasure.

Carter trusted her logistics so much that he assumed she was a robot who could schedule around suicide. Keela was treating her labor like a service she was entitled to review on Yelp.

She wiped her wet hands on a towel. She reached for her pocket. *Calculator+*.

Amara: *I am invisible. Carter is drinking wine and at me about a suit. Keela calls me aggressive because I'm cooking her dinner. I am suffocating in my own kitchen. I want to burn the peppers.*

She waited. She stared at the screen, blocking out Carter's voice describing the fit of the gray jacket.

Darius: *You are vivid. You are the woman whose life was saved with frozen kale. You met an incredible dude like me and made him love. Do not apologize. Do not pick out the peppers. Walk away. Let the Utility fail.*

Amara took a deep breath. She looked at the pile of chopped peppers. She looked at Carter. She looked at Keela.

"I'm experiencing inflammation," Amara announced flatly.

The room went silent.

"What?" Carter asked. "Like... arthritis?"

"No," Amara said. "Spiritual inflammation. The vibe is toxic."

She put the knife down. She untied her apron and dropped it on the island.

"I'm going to the Attic."

"The Attic?" Carter frowned, looking at the half-chopped vegetables. "But... dinner? The stove is on."

"There is pasta in the pantry," Amara said. "There is water in the tap. And the dry cleaner is open until seven. You have a car, Carter. You have a license."

"But I'm prepping for the meeting!"

"And I," Amara said, walking past him, "am prepping for survival."

She walked out. She climbed the stairs to the Attic, the wood creaking under her boots. She sat in her chair, wrapped herself in a blanket, and put on her noise-canceling headphones. She played Coltrane.

Downstairs, the silence was heavy. She knew there was this muffled confusion, the sounds of a system crashing as the server went offline.

Amara: *I walked out. They look confused. The stir-fry is abandoned.*

Darius: *Good. Let them figure out the geometry of a noodle. Stay in the Attic.*

Part III: The Breach (The Close Call)

Thursday Night. The Bedroom.

Amara was in bed, propped up against the pillows. It was 10:30 PM. Carter was in the en-suite bathroom, flossing with a rhythmic snapping sound that made Amara want to commit a felony.

She had her iPad on her lap. To the naked eye, she was checking Zillow, fantasizing about mid-century modern homes in remote locations. But underneath the Zillow tab, *Calculator+* was open. She was midway through composing a draft about the way the rain sounded on the roof.

Snap. Snap. Snap.

Carter walked out of the bathroom. He was wearing his "sensible" pajamas—cotton plaid, ironed. He smelled of mint and moral superiority.

"Hey," he said, walking toward her side of the bed. "I need to find that photo of the kids from the Cape Cod trip. The one where Marcus is holding the crab. I want to use it for the 'Family Values' slide in the quarterly all-hands project."

"It's on the cloud," Amara said, not looking up. She quickly double-tapped the home button, swiping the calculator app away, but her thumb slipped. The screen froze for a microsecond.

"I can't find it on mine," Carter said. He reached out.

It was a casual, proprietary gesture. He didn't ask. He just reached for the device in her hands as if it were a toaster or a remote control—a piece of household infrastructure he owned.

"Let me check yours. You organize the albums better."

His hand touched the corner of the iPad.

Amara lunged.

It wasn't a gentle pull. It was a visceral, defensive recoil. She yanked the iPad against her chest, her knuckles turning white.

"Don't," she snapped.

The word was sharp, louder than she intended. It cracked the domestic silence like a whip.

Carter froze, his hand hovering in mid-air. He looked at her, his expression shifting from mild annoyance to genuine confusion.

"Woah," he said, stepping back. "Easy. I just need the photo."

"I am using it," Amara said. Her heart was hammering against her ribs like a trapped bird. "I am... looking at houses."

"Okay..." Carter narrowed his eyes. "But why did you jump like that? You acted like I was grabbing a live wire."

"Because," Amara said, struggling to steady her voice, "you assume access, Carter. You always assume access. You reach for my time, you reach for my labor, and now you're reaching for my screen without asking. It's... it's intrusive."

Carter stared at her. He looked hurt. But underneath the hurt, there was suspicion.

"It's an iPad, Amara. I pay the data plan."

"You pay for the hardware, and I pay the note on this house, so what's your point?" Amara countered, clutching the device tighter. "You don't own the thoughts."

Carter looked at her for a long moment. He looked at the device pressed to her chest. He looked at the flush on her neck.

"You're acting weird," he muttered. "You've been weird since you got back. Like you're hoarding yourself."

"Maybe I am," Amara whispered. "Maybe there wasn't much left to hoard."

Carter sighed—the heavy, disappointed sigh of a man who found the vending machine empty. He turned off the lamp on his side.

"Fine. Send me the photo in the morning. If you can spare the bandwidth."

He climbed into bed and turned his back to her.

Amara sat in the dark, the iPad burning against her chest. She waited until his breathing evened out into the soft, rhythmic snoring of the righteous.

She opened *Calculator+*. Her hands were shaking.

Amara: *He tried to take the iPad. He touched it. I almost bit him. I physically yanked it away. He knows something is wrong. He called me a hoarder.*

Darius: *You are a hoarder. You are hoarding your soul. It is your most valuable asset. Guard it with your life. I'm putting a kill switch on the app just in case.*

Amara: *It was close, Darius. Too close.*

Darius: *I know. Keep the device locked. Keep the heart locked. I've got you.*

Part IV: The Drag

Friday Night. Atlanta.

The Dinner Party was Sasha's idea. It was always Sasha's idea.

She had invited her "circle"—a group of five women who were all varying degrees of influencers, life coaches, or brand ambassadors. They sat in the living room, drinking skinny margaritas that tasted like lime juice and ambition.

Darius sat in the corner armchair, holding a hardcover copy of *Invisible Man* as a shield. He was wearing the costume—slacks, sweater, smile—but his eyes were dead.

"Honestly," Sasha said, pitching her voice up for her friends, "it's just so hard. I tried to do a 'Welcome Home' reel when he got back from his... *retreat*... and he literally walked out of the frame. He's so moody lately."

The friends giggled. A chorus of sympathetic vibrations.

"Men are such projects," one said, a woman named Bethany who sold essential oils she claimed cured anxiety. "You have to mold them. It's like pottery."

"Right?" Sasha sighed, swirling her glass. "He just doesn't get the vision. He's very... analog. He thinks privacy is a virtue. Can you imagine?"

"So retro," Bathany agreed. "If you don't post it, did it even happen?"

Darius kept his head down. He typed under the cover of the book.

Darius: *She is doing the 'moody husband' routine. I am a project. I am analog. She is apologizing for my existence to women who sell oils.*

Amara: *Drag her. Use the British method. Smile while you cut. Do not let them treat you like furniture.*

Darius felt a smile twitch at the corner of his mouth. He closed his book with a heavy *thud*.

"Actually, Sasha," Darius said. His voice cut through the chatter like a knife through silk.

The room went silent. Five pairs of perfectly lashed eyes turned to him.

"I wasn't walking out of the frame because I was moody," he said, his voice calm, reasonable, almost helpful. "I walked out because the ring light washes out the architectural details of the basement. I was protecting your production value."

Sasha blinked. "Oh. Well—"

"And regarding the 'vision,'" Darius continued, turning his gaze to Bethany. He smiled. It was a shark's smile. "I think it's adorable how hard you all work on your... digital scrapbooking."

The air left the room.

"Digital... scrapbooking?" Bethany whispered, clutching her pearls.

"Is that not the term?" Darius asked innocently. "My apologies. 'Content creation.' It's very... spirited. It's charming, really. To see you treating the algorithm like it's a career. It keeps you busy. It keeps you out of the way with the two followers you have—"

He stood up. He adjusted his sweater.

"I'm going to the Fortress. Enjoy the margaritas. I believe the lime juice is fresh. Maybe when ya'll take off and make some loot, I cna stop funding this shit."

He walked calmly to the basement door, punched in the code, and locked it behind him.

Darius: *I called it "digital scrapbooking." I called them "spirited." The silence was deafening. I think I killed the party.*

Amara: *Spirited! Oh my god. That is lethal. I am laughing so hard Dung-Chul is barking. You are an assassin.*

Darius: *I learned from the best. I wore the costume, but I held the match.*

Part V: The Midnight Synod (The Deep Night)

3:00 AM. The Void.

The adrenaline of the day had faded. The house was quiet. Amara couldn't sleep. The close call with Carter had left her vibrating with a residual panic.

She logged into ProtonMail. There was already a draft waiting.

Subject: System Update (Saved Draft)

I sneezed in the shower tonight. Just a normal sneeze. And I pulled a muscle in my lower back that I didn't even know existed. I am currently lying on the floor of the server room because the cold concrete is the only thing that helps. I am a technological genius, Amara, and I have been defeated by a sneeze.

Amara laughed into her pillow. The sound was wet, half-sob, half-giggle. She typed back.

I found a chin hair today. Not a polite, peach-fuzz hair. A structural hair. A load-bearing hair. I tried to pluck it and my skin just laughed at me. I realized that my body is slowly turning into a haunted house.

She saved it. Watched the screen refresh.

A haunted house is interesting. Better than an open house. Better than a staged property.

Amara, do you ever worry that we missed the boat?

The tone shifted. The humor evaporated, leaving the raw substrate of 3:00 AM honesty.

What do you mean? she typed.

I mean the 'Living' part. I feel like I spent the last twenty years reading the manual and assembling the furniture, but I never actually sat in the chair. And now my back hurts, and I have gray in my beard, and I'm wondering if the warranty has expired.

Amara stared at the cursor blinking in the dark. It was the fear she kept tucked behind her ribcage. The fear that this—the affair, the connection, the awakening—was just a flare before the dark.

The warranty is void, she wrote back. *We broke the seal in the cabin. But Darius? I don't want a refund.*

I'm not afraid of the gray. I'm not afraid of the chin hair (well, mostly). I'm afraid of the smoothness. I'm afraid of sliding into the grave without a single scratch on the paint.

We aren't aging out of relevance. We are aging into substance.

Your back hurts because you're carrying the weight of being real in a fake world.

She paused.

Also, try Ibuprofen and a foam roller. I'm a doctor (sort of).

She hit save.

A moment later, a new line appeared.

Yes, Doctor. I'll get the roller.

And Amara? Scratches on the paint. That's the goal. Let's wreck the car.

Part VI: The Promise

The next morning, the resolve was hardened. The ongoing fear of being caught by Carter, the exhaustion of the performance, the existential dread of the "Deep Night"—it all coalesced into a single data point.

They needed a physical server. The cloud wasn't enough.

Darius refreshed the page one last time before the sun hit the basement windows.

Subject: Seattle (Saved Draft)

I looked at the calendar. There is a summit in Seattle next month. "The Intersection of Technology and Human Behavior."

It fits your work. It fits mine. I can get a speaking slot. Carter won't question it. He respects conferences. Conferences are tax-deductible.

I can book a suite at the Hyatt. Room 303.

Darius stared at the screen. A hotel. A suite. Room service. It sounded easy. It sounded safe.

He began to type, his fingers flying over the keys.

Subject: Re: Seattle (Saved Draft)

No.

I can't do a hotel, Amara. I can't do beige walls and room service and pretending to be professional in the elevator. I don't want to meet you in a lobby. I don't want to check in.

I want to meet you in the quiet.

The conference is the cover. But it's not the destination.

He hit refresh. He waited. The fan of his server rack whirred.

Subject: The Sanctuary (Saved Draft)

I checked the rental site. The Olympic Peninsula. The road is clear. Cabin Two is available.

And so is Cabin One. I'm booking them both. I'll tell Carter I'm going to the conference for a week to write my paper on "Digital Erasure."

You tell Sasha you're speaking at the summit. Fly into SeaTac. Rent a car. Drive west.

I'll meet you where the road ends.

Darius closed his eyes. He could smell the rain. He could feel the ghost of her hand on his chest. He could hear the wind singing through the trees.

He typed one last line.

Subject: The Return (Saved Draft)

It's done. March 14th. I'll bring the tea. You bring the Coltrane. We're going home.

He saved it. He closed the laptop.

Upstairs, his wife was scrolling TikTok, looking for validation. Downstairs, Darius was planning an escape.

CHAPTER 8: THE SECOND RETREAT (3 MONTHS LATER)

Part I: The Breaking Point

Atlanta. March 12th.

The breaking point didn't sound like a scream. It sounded like a text message notification pinging repeatedly against a granite countertop, like a drop of water that eventually erodes a canyon.

Darius sat at his kitchen island, attempting to eat a bowl of oatmeal that had turned to the consistency of wet cement. Across from him, the Twins—Mike and Bea—were vibrating with the specific, terrifying energy of teenagers who had just realized their own market value.

"Dad," Mike said, shoving an iPhone screen into Darius's face. The brightness was set to 100%. "Look at the torque."

Darius blinked, leaning back. "I am eating oatmeal, Mike. I don't want to look at torque."

"It's a G-Wagon, Dad," Bea chimed in, not looking up from her own phone where she was scrolling through customized license plate options. "It's safety. It's basically a tank. Do you want us to die in a Honda?"

"I want you to live in reality," Darius said, pushing the phone away gently. "You are turning seventeen. You are getting a vehicle that gets you from Point A to Point B. You are not getting a vehicle that requires a military clearance to operate."

"Mom said you'd say that," Bea sighed, a sound that managed to convey disappointment, exhaustion, and pity all at once. "She said you have a scarcity mindset because of your 'generational trauma.'"

Darius stopped chewing. He looked at his daughter. He looked at the pristine, white-marble kitchen that cost more than the house he grew up in. He looked at the untouched espresso machine.

"My scarcity mindset," Darius repeated slowly, "is the reason you are wearing sneakers that cost four hundred dollars."

"Okay, boomer," Mike muttered, swiping to the next photo. "Anyway, this one has matte black rims. It's sick."

The phone pinged again. Sasha.

Text: Can you handle the caterer for the birthday party? They need a deposit. I'm at the studio.

Ping.

Text: Also, the pool guy says the filter is cracked. Can you call him?

Ping.

Text: Mike really wants the G-Wagon. Maybe we lease it?

Darius stared at the phone. He stared at his children, who were currently discussing whether "LIT-AF" was an appropriate license plate.

The noise in the room wasn't loud—it was the hum of the refrigerator, the tap of thumbs on glass, the drone of entitlement—but it felt deafening. It felt like the air was being sucked out of the room, replaced by a vacuum of demands.

Darius stood up. He picked up his bowl of oatmeal. He walked to the trash can and scraped it in.

"Dad?" Bea asked. "Where are you going?"

"I have a conference," Darius said. He didn't look back. "In Seattle."

"When?"

"Now."

Portland. March 12th.

Amara was sitting in the master bathroom, or what used to be the master bathroom. Currently, it was a demolition zone wrapped in plastic sheeting.

Carter stood in the center of the room, holding a tape measure like a weapon. He was wearing a headlamp, even though it was 2:00 PM on a Saturday and the sun was shining.

"The issue," Carter said, for the fourth time, "is the grout line. If we go with the 12-by-24 tiles, the grout line will intersect with the drain at an asymmetrical angle. It will look chaotic, Amara."

Amara sat on the closed toilet lid—the only surface not covered in dust. She was holding a book, *The Body Keeps the Score*, but she hadn't turned a page in twenty minutes.

"Chaotic," she repeated dullly.

"Yes. Visually disturbing. I've modeled it in SketchUp," Carter said, tapping the iPad propped up on the sink vanity. "Option A puts the drain in the center, but we lose two inches of clearance on the shower door. Option B keeps the clearance, but the grout line... well, look."

He gestured to the screen. Amara didn't look. She looked at Carter.

She looked at the way he was vibrating with anxiety over a millimeter of grout. She looked at the way he had turned their home into a project, a series of problems to be optimized, rather than a place to live.

"Carter," she said softy.

"And don't get me started on the fixtures," he continued, pacing the small room, the plastic sheeting crinkling around him. "Brushed nickel is timeless, but matte black is trending. But if we do matte black, we have to change the hinges on the door. It's a cascade failure."

"Carter."

"What?" He spun around, the headlamp blinding her momentarily.

"I don't care about the grout," she said.

Carter froze. He looked hurt. He looked like she had just told him she didn't care about democracy.

"You don't care? Amara, we live here. This affects the resale value. This affects the *flow*."

"I don't care about the flow," she whispered. "I care about the noise."

"What noise? The contractors aren't here today."

"The noise in here," she tapped her chest. "It's screaming, Carter. You are screaming about tile, and Keela is screaming about her essay, and the house is screaming to be fixed, and I just..."

She stood up. She felt lightheaded.

"I need to go."

"Go where? To the store? We need to pick the tile."

"Seattle," she said. It was a reflex. A password.

"Seattle? For what? The conference was three months ago."

"Follow-up summit," Amara lied. The lie tasted sweet. It tasted like oxygen. "Technology and... Human Resilience."

She walked out of the bathroom, leaving him standing there with his tape measure extended, trying to quantify the distance between them.

Part II: The Arrival

Cabin One. The Olympic Peninsula.

Darius arrived first.

The rental car—a nondescript Chevy Malibu that lacked torque but possessed anonymity—crunched over the gravel driveway of Cabin One. The sound was distinct: the popping of rocks under rubber, followed by the immediate, heavy silence of the forest.

He killed the engine.

He didn't get out immediately. He sat there, hands on the wheel, waiting for the ringing in his ears to stop. It was the phantom ringing of the Atlanta airport, of the twins' demands, of Sasha's "peace" candles burning in the foyer.

He took a breath. He held it. He let it out.

The air outside the car was different. He could see the mist clinging to the windows. He stepped out.

The silence hit him like a physical weight. It wasn't empty; it was dense. It was a silence made of millions of pine needles absorbing the sound, of moss dampening the earth, of the lake swallowing the light.

He unpacked slowly. This was part of the ritual now.

He carried his leather duffel into the main room. He set up the turntable on the sideboard. He placed the stack of vinyl—Coltrane, Miles Davis, Bill Evans—next to it.

He put the bottle of Pinot Noir on the counter to breathe.

He opened the back door and stepped onto the porch. The cold air bit through his flannel shirt, sharp and clean. It smelled of wet cedar and ozone.

He sat in the Adirondack chair. And he waited.

This was the hardest part. The transition. The "Bends."

He checked his watch. 4:15 PM.

She said she was driving down in the afternoon.

Darius stared at the tree line separating Cabin One from Cabin Two. It was a thicket of ferns and hemlock, dense and shadowy. There was a narrow footpath cutting through it—a deer trail they had claimed as their own.

He felt the old itch of anxiety, the "Prop" instinct kicking in. *What if she doesn't come? What if Carter guilted her into staying to pick grout? What if the reality of the lie was too heavy this time?*

He forced himself to stay seated. He forced himself not to check his phone.

4:30 PM. The wind picked up, rustling the tops of the firs.

4:45 PM. A squirrel skittered across the railing, chattering loudly.

5:15 PM. A branch snapped.

It was a sharp, dry crack that sliced through the quiet. Darius's hand tightened on the armrest.

He saw a splash of color between the trees. Yellow.

Amara emerged from the forest. She was looking down, watching her footing on the slick roots, her brow furrowed in concentration. She was wearing a bright yellow raincoat that looked like a beacon in the gray gloom. Her hood was pushed back, her curls damp and frizzing in the mist.

She was carrying a canvas tote bag over one shoulder and a bottle of wine in the other hand.

She looked exhausted. She looked stripped down. She looked real.

She stopped at the edge of the clearing. She lifted her head.

When she saw him sitting there, she stopped. Her shoulders dropped three inches. The tension that had been holding her upright seemed to dissolve, leaving her soft.

"I parked at the other cabin," she called out. Her voice was slightly breathless. "The driveway was muddy," as she moved her braids back.

Darius smiled. It wasn't a camera-ready smile. It was a smile that started in his chest.

"I thought you stood me up," he called back, standing up.

"I thought about it," she admitted, stepping toward the porch stairs. "Somewhere around Olympia. I thought, 'I am a terrible mother. I am abandoning my family for a weekend of Scrabble.'"

She climbed the steps, mud streaking her boots.

"And then?" Darius asked.

"Then I remembered you have the good wine," she said. "And Carter asked me if I preferred 'Arctic White' or 'Dover White' grout."

She reached the top step. She dropped her bag.

She stepped into his space.

It wasn't a collision this time. It wasn't the desperate, starving grasp of the first retreat. It was an arrival.

She wrapped her arms around his waist, burying her face in the flannel of his shirt. He wrapped his arms around her, pulling her in, resting his chin on the top of her head.

She smelled of rain, bariad oil, and the peppermint mints she kept in her pocket.

"You made it," he murmured into her hair.

"We made it," she corrected, her voice muffled against his chest.

They stood there for a long time, just holding each other up, letting the silence of the forest stitch them back together.

Part III: The Exhale

The intimacy was different this time.

In the winter, during the storm, it had been urgent—a frantic need to prove they were alive. It had been about heat and friction and breaking the seal on twenty years of loneliness.

This time, it was an exhale.

The bedroom of Cabin One was dim, lit only by the gray light filtering through the linen curtains. The rain had started up again, a soft drumming on the roof that sealed them in.

They moved together with a slow, deliberate rhythm. There was no rushing. There was no performance.

Darius traced the line of her spine with his palm, learning the map of her tension. Amara kissed the hollow of his throat, tasting the salt and the skin.

It was the kind of intimacy where you didn't suck in your stomach. You didn't worry about the angle of your chin. You didn't worry about the noise you made.

At one point, Darius tried to shift his weight to pull the duvet up, and his elbow slipped off the edge of the mattress. His arm flailed, knocking the nightstand lamp, which wobbled precariously before he caught it.

"Whoops," he yelped, a high-pitched, undignified sound.

In Atlanta, he would have been mortified. He would have apologized. He would have ruined the mood.

Here, Amara started to laugh.

It started as a giggle against his neck and bloomed into a full-body shake. She laughed until she was gasping, her forehead pressed into his chest.

"Smooth," she wheezed. "Very 007."

"Occupational hazard," Darius groaned, laughing with her, pulling her back down. "I've been compromised. The infrastructure is failing."

"Man down," she whispered, kissing his shoulder. "Medic required."

"I think I need mouth-to-mouth," he said.

"I think you need a helmet."

They lay there afterward, tangled in sheets that smelled of cedar and detergent. The light shifted across the ceiling, turning from gray to a deep, bruised blue.

They talked about everything and nothing. They talked about the water pressure (better here than at home). They talked about the weird shape of the pinecones outside. They talked about the twins' G-Wagon demands and Carter's grout obsession.

"It's nice," Amara whispered, tracing the scar on his shoulder with her finger. "Being boring with you."

"We're not boring," Darius murmured, catching her hand and kissing her knuckles. "We're efficient. We're maximizing the chill. Hey, where is Dung-Chul?"

"He is at the cabin enjoying himself. I don't think he wanted to come this time," she laughs. "If he misses us, I'm sure he will come. So, are we efficient? Is that what the kids say?"

"The kids say 'Lit AF'," Darius said grimly. "We are definitely not that."

"Thank God," Amara said. She closed her eyes. "I love boring. Boring is a luxury."

Part IV: Parallel Play

The next day, they didn't cling. They didn't hover. The panic of separation—the fear that if they looked away, the other would vanish—was gone.

They reclaimed the selves they had forgotten.

Cabin Two: The Release

Amara set up her easel on the back deck of Cabin Two. The air was cool, biting at her cheeks, but she didn't put on a coat. She wore one of Darius's oversized flannel shirts, the sleeves rolled up past her elbows.

She squeezed the paint directly onto the palette. Not sensible colors. Not "Dover White" or "Arctic White."

She used violent oranges. Deep, bruised purples. A crimson so dark it looked like blood.

She didn't use a brush at first. She used her fingers. She smeared the color across the canvas, feeling the texture of the oil paint, the drag of the linen. It was messy. It was tactile.

She wasn't painting a landscape. She was painting the noise in her head. She was painting the scream she hadn't let out in the bathroom with Carter.

She worked for three hours without stopping. She got paint in her hair. She got paint on her chin. She didn't check her phone. She didn't check the time.

She just let it out.

Cabin One: The Logic

Darius sat on the porch of Cabin One, his laptop warm against his thighs. The smell of damp wood rose around him.

He wasn't checking email. He wasn't managing a team. He wasn't putting out fires.

He was coding. Just for the joy of it.

He was building a useless, beautiful little app that connected to the local weather station's API. He wrote a script that translated wind speed into sound.

He sat there, typing lines of Python, feeling the satisfying click of the keys, the order of the syntax. *If this, then that.*

The world was chaotic, but code was clean. Code obeyed him.

He tested it.

Ping. A light breeze registered as a high C.

Bong. A gust registered as a low G.

It blended with the natural soundscape—the wind through the branches, the distant water lapping against the shore. It created a strange, accidental symphony.

Around 2:00 PM, he walked the trail to check on her. He found her standing back from the easel, covered in blue and orange streaks. She looked like she had wrestled a rainbow and won.

"What is that noise?" Amara asked, wiping her hands on a rag. "I keep hearing bells."

"It's the wind," Darius said, leaning against the railing, grinning. "I gave it a voice. Every time the wind shifts, it sings."

"It sounds like a zen garden having a panic attack," she said, narrowing her eyes at him.

"It's atmospheric," he insisted. "It's generative art, Amara. You wouldn't understand. You're too busy finger-painting."

"It's Abstract Expressionism," she retorted, dipping a brush into the red. "And your app is annoying. It's interrupting my angst."

"You love it."

"I tolerate it," she smiled. "Because you look happy."

"I am," he said. And he realized it was true.

Dung-chul trotted out onto the deck the second he heard Darius, tail already doing helicopter rotations. The moment he spotted Darius, he let out one triumphant bark — the kind that said *Oh good, the tall one who makes her happy is back.*

Before Darius could protest, the dog pressed his whole golden body against his legs, sniffing him like he was checking for contraband.

"Relax," Darius muttered, stiff as a lamppost. "I'm not here for you."

Dung-chul ignored that lie completely and nudged his hand with the force of a small SUV.

Darius sighed, gave him a good pat down, and the dog melted like butter in a cast-iron skillet.

"Unbelievable," Darius said, but he didn't stop petting him.

Part V: The Union

Lunch was sandwiches on the shared dock. The sun had broken through the clouds—a rare March gift—warming the wood beneath them.

The lake smelled clean and metallic. The water was still, reflecting the dark green of the firs.

They sat side by side, legs dangling over the edge, boots nearly touching the water.

Darius ate a turkey club that Amara had made. She had remembered he liked heavy mustard. She had remembered he hated tomatoes.

Amara ate an apple, the crunch echoing across the water.

"We need a name," Amara said, watching a mallard duck land with a soft splash near the reeds.

"For the duck?" Darius asked, mouth full.

"No, Darius. For this. For us." She gestured between them, then to the cabins behind them.

"We can't keep calling it 'The Glitch' or 'The Affair.' It feels too... scandalous. This doesn't feel scandalous. It feels like a medical necessity. Like dialysis."

Darius chewed thoughtfully. He looked at her—paint in her hair, relaxation in her shoulders, the "Utility" offline.

"A union," he said.

Amara laughed. "We're not a union. We don't have dues."

"Don't we?" Darius countered. "We pay dues every day back there. Emotional tax. Heavy lifting. Management fees."

He nudged her shoulder with his.

"Feels like a labor union to me. Two overworked employees are finally organizing against management."

Amara smiled. She liked the weight of it. She liked the unromantic, practical solidity of it.

"The Union," she said softly. "Local 303."

"Why 303?"

"That was the room number of the first hotel we didn't go to. In Seattle. The one with the beige walls."

"Fair," Darius said. "Local 303."

He raised his sandwich in a toast. "To collective bargaining."

Amara tapped her apple against his crust. "To breaks."

"To strictly enforced downtime."

"To the right to remain silent about the dishwasher."

They ate in companionable silence, watching the water ripple. The name settled around them like a coat.

The Union.

Not a secret society. Not a betrayal. A protective organization.

A pact that said: *When the world tries to turn us into functions, we come here to be human.*

The wind picked up, rustling the reeds. From the direction of Cabin One, faint and melodic, came a soft *bing-bong* from Darius's laptop speakers.

"Your app is working," Amara murmured, leaning her head on his shoulder.

"Our app," Darius corrected. "Union property."

Amara laughed—a low, rich sound that startled the duck into flight. She closed her eyes, listening to the wind singing through Darius's code, and felt entirely, wonderfully useless.

The sun dipped lower. The air grew colder. But they didn't move. They sat there on the edge of the world, two members of the smallest, quietest union on earth, holding the line.

CHAPTER 9: THE NON-AGGRESSION PACT

The rain on the Olympic Peninsula didn't fall; it negotiated. It started as a mist, a polite suggestion that you might want to stay indoors. Then it upgraded to a drizzle, a persistent, rhythmic tapping that tested the integrity of your roof. And finally, around 9:00 PM, it became a deluge—a heavy, vertical curtain of water that turned the world outside Cabin Four into a gray, aquatic blur.

Inside, the air smelled of cedar, wet wool, and the specific, tannic bite of a twenty-dollar bottle of Pinot Noir that Darius had found at the general store. The fire in the hearth wasn't roaring; it was muttering, occasionally spitting a spark of protest against the damp draft coming down the chimney.

Darius sat on one side of the small, scarred oak table. Amara sat on the other.

Between them lay a Scrabble board.

It was a battlefield.

Darius had seven tiles on his rack. He rearranged them with the obsessive precision of a man who used to organize server blades for a living. *C-O-D-E-R-S*. No. Too cheap. *S-C-O-R-E-D*. Better. But he needed to land on the Double Word Score to clear the deficit.

He looked up. Amara was staring at the board, her chin resting in her hand. She was wearing a bulky gray sweater that looked like it had been knitted by a blind sailor, and she looked entirely, terrifyingly comfortable.

"You're overthinking it," she said, without looking at him. Her voice had that slight, clipped precision that usually only came out when she was annoyed or winning.

"I'm strategizing," Darius corrected. "There's a difference."

"The difference is about three minutes," she said. "Play the word, Darius. The wine is breathing faster than you are."

Darius placed his tiles. **Q-U-I-E-T.** The 'Q' landed on a Triple Letter score.

"Thirty-four points," he announced, leaning back in the creaky wooden chair.

Amara looked at the word. She took a sip of her wine. "Subtle."

"I thought so."

She reached for her tiles. She didn't hesitate. She didn't rearrange. She just laid them down, intersecting his 'T' with a vertical precision that felt surgical.

T-R-A-U-M-A.

Darius stared at the board. "Trauma? Really?"

"It's a valid word," she said, marking the score on a napkin. "And it's worth twelve points. Plus the fifty-point bonus for using all seven letters. That's sixty-two."

She smiled. It wasn't a nice smile. It was the smile of a woman who had spent twenty years listening to other people's problems and had finally decided to win a game.

"You're a shark," Darius said, refilling his mug.

"I'm a therapist," she corrected. "Same skill set, less swimming."

They had been in the cabin for three hours. The initial awkwardness—the "what are we doing here" energy—had dissolved into the easy rhythm of two people who were equally done with the world.

Darius watched her pick up her wine glass. She held it differently than Sasha did. Sasha held a wine glass like it was a prop in a photo shoot—fingers elongated, stem poised. Amara held it like it was fuel.

"You sounded different just now," Darius noted. "When you told me to hurry up. You sounded... British."

Amara paused. She set the glass down. "Did I? It slips out when I'm impatient. Or intoxicated. Or dealing with American inefficiency."

"I knew it," Darius said, pointing a pretzel at her. "I knew there was an accent buried under the NPR voice. How long have you been here?"

"In the States?" Amara calculated, looking at the ceiling. "Twenty-two years. I came for a Master's program in Boston and never left. I got trapped by the portion sizes and the illusion of upward mobility."

"Twenty-two years," Darius whistled. "That's a life sentence."

"It feels like it sometimes," she admitted. "But I still dream in metric. And I still think your tea is an act of violence."

Darius laughed. "Our tea? You mean Lipton?"

"I mean the lukewarm brown water you people serve in restaurants," she said, shuddering. "It's aggressive. It's disrespectful to the leaf."

"Okay, Duchess," Darius teased. "So, break it down for me. You've got twenty years of data. UK Blacks versus American Blacks. Who's got it worse?"

Amara groaned, leaning back in her chair. "Oh, God. The Diaspora Wars. Are we really doing this?"

"We are," Darius said. "I need to know. I've seen *Luther*. I've seen *Top Boy*. You guys look cool. You wear turtlenecks and solve crimes in brooding silence. We just... march."

Amara laughed, a sharp, barking sound. "It's not that simple, Darius. It's a different *texture* of racism."

"Explain the texture."

Amara spun her wine glass by the stem. "Okay. In the UK? The racism is polite. It's quiet. It's a look in a shop. It's a question about where you're *really* from, asked over a biscuit. It's gaslighting. You spend half your life wondering if you imagined it."

"And here?"

"Here?" She gestured to the window, to the dark American woods. "Here, it's loud. It's high-definition. American racism has a marketing budget. It's on the news at 6:00, 7:00, and 11:00. It doesn't hide. It pulls you over and asks for your license."

"So you prefer the gaslighting?"

"I prefer the tea," she deflected. "But honestly? The biggest difference is the exhaustion. American Black folks are tired in a way that feels... cellular. You guys carry the soil's history. In London, we carry the history of the Empire, but we can technically 'go back' somewhere in our heads. Even if we've never been there. You guys *are* here. There's nowhere to go back to."

Darius nodded slowly. He felt that. The cellular fatigue. The weight of being the default setting for "The Struggle."

"Plus," Amara added, "there's the 'Black Nod.'"

"The Nod is universal," Darius argued.

"It is," she agreed. "But the American Nod is different. In London, the Nod says, 'I see you. We are both outnumbered. Cheerio.' In America, the Nod says, 'I see you. Are we safe? Do you know where the exit is? Good luck.'"

Darius chuckled, but it was a dark sound. "That's accurate. It's a survival check."

"Exactly. And don't get me started on the 'Magic Negro' trope," she said, picking up a Scrabble tile. "Americans love a Magical Negro. The wise, suffering saint who helps the White protagonist find their car keys and their soul. In the UK, we're usually just the villain or the sidekick who dies first."

"I'd rather be the villain," Darius mused. "Villains get better wardrobes. And, I ain't marching for nobody no more. I'm minding my Black ass business until they clear all that trash out of the house. Be marching for Latinos and the call you the N-word behind your back. These folks love our culture, but not us, and the Black folks get a little money and think they made it. I am exhausted. Minding ny business works."

"And better hours," Amara agreed. "Being a saint is a 24/7 gig. No overtime pay."

The conversation lulled, but it wasn't empty. It was filled with the crackle of the fire and the drumming rain.

Darius poured the last of the wine into their mismatched mugs. His said *World's Okayest Golfer*. Hers was red and chipped.

"I haven't checked my phone in six hours," Darius said, watching the dark liquid swirl. "I don't know who's trending. I don't know what crisis is happening on social media. It feels... illegal."

Amara laughed, low in her throat. "I know. I usually spend my evenings doom-scrolling until my retinas detach. It's my penance."

"Not anymore," Darius said. He took a long drink, feeling the warmth spread through his chest. "I'm done. I officially retired last Tuesday."

"Retired from work?"

"No. From the *struggle*," Darius said. He waved a hand vaguely at the window, toward the rest of the continent. "I realized something after this last election. I watched the returns come in. I watched the pundits hyperventilate. And I had an epiphany."

"Which was?"

"The White folks? They got it."

Amara choked on her wine. She put the mug down, wiping her mouth with the back of her hand, eyes wide with amusement. "Excuse me?"

"They got it," Darius repeated, his voice level and deadly serious. "I am stepping down from the Board of Directors of Saving Democracy. I'm handing over the keys. You want to run it into the ditch? Go ahead. Drive it off the cliff. I'll be in the backseat with a neck pillow and some noise-canceling headphones."

Amara threw her head back and laughed—a real, full-bodied laugh that shook the table and made the Scrabble tiles rattle. "Oh my god. I thought it was just me. I looked at the exit polls and said, 'Welp, looks like a systemic issue. Good luck with that. I am doing a Clarity of Absence."

"Exactly," Darius said, leaning in. "Why are we stressing? We didn't build the machine. Why are we trying to fix the gears while it's chewing off our arms?"

"It's the guilt," Amara said, wiping a tear from her eye. "It's the ancestral guilt. Harriet Tubman walked so I could drive a Subaru, so I feel like I have to drive the Subaru to a protest."

"Harriet walked so you could take a *nap*," Darius corrected. "That's the part they leave out of the history books. She wanted to rest, Amara."

"I'm tired, Darius," she confessed, her laughter fading into a weary smile. "I'm tired of the outrage. I'm tired of the panels. And you know who I'm really tired of?"

"Who?"

"The talking Black folks," Darius said, answering for her. "The Professional Explainers. We talked about this before, but I've really been thinking about it. Your husband is White so I know you tired."

Amara pointed a finger at him. "You're funny! Yes! The ones on cable news. The ones in the crisp suits who go on the tele and use words like 'intersectionality' and 'paradigm shift' and 'the Black body.' They sound so good. They sound so smooth. But they aren't *doing* anything. They're just remixing the struggle for a paycheck."

"Eloquence without infrastructure," Darius nodded. "I know them. I see them at tech summits. They get paid ten grand to give a keynote on 'Diversity as a Driver of Innovation,' and then they go home to a gated community and ignore their cousins."

"I work with them," Amara said. "In academia? It's an epidemic. They write fifty-page papers on equity, but they won't hold the elevator for the janitor. They treat 'Blackness' like a tenure track requirement, not a life."

"I'm done with it," Darius declared. "I don't want to be an activist. I don't want to be a 'voice.' I just want to be a guy who pays his taxes, hates his HOA, and drinks Pinot Noir in a cabin that smells like burning wood."

"I resigned as a 'Strong Black Woman' three days ago," Amara said softly. "I sent a mental resignation letter to the ancestors. I said, 'Thank you for the opportunity, but I would like to pivot to being a Mediocre Black Woman who makes bad financial decisions."

"Did they accept it?"

"Pending review," she grinned. "But I'm acting like it's approved."

The fire popped again, sending a flare of light across the room. The shadows danced on the walls—long, distorted shapes that looked like ghosts.

"What about the spouses?" Amara asked. "Do they get it?"

Darius sighed. He pictured Sasha. "Sasha thinks 'The Struggle' is a hashtag. She thinks posting a black square is activism. She asked me once if we should 'march for the brand.' I think she meant it earnestly."

"Carter," Amara said, shaking her head, "Carter thinks racism is a market inefficiency. He thinks that if we just get enough credit scores over 750, the police will stop shooting us. He's optimizing his time with a Black woman."

"Does it work?"

"No. He just doesn't get it, and I'm tired of explaining. It's even harder now that I am with a premium Black man."

"That sounds like a stereotype," he jokes.

"It is."

They both laughed, but it was the quiet, knowing laughter of people who had been having the same argument with their partners for a decade.

"I love him," Amara said, tracing the grain of the wooden table. "I really do. But he's exhausting. He's so... logical. He thinks everything has a solution. He doesn't understand that some things just *are*."

"Sasha is the opposite," Darius said. "She thinks everything is a vibe. If the vibe is off, we fix it with sage. If the world is burning, we curate the smoke."

"We're the shock absorbers," Amara said. "That's what we are. You absorb Sasha's chaos. I absorb Carter's rigidity. We take the hit so they can keep functioning."

"And who absorbs us?" Darius asked.

Amara looked at him. The question hung in the air, heavy and unanswered.

"Nobody," she whispered. "That's why we're here."

The rain intensified, hammering against the roof as if trying to break in. But inside, the circle of light from the fire felt safe. It felt fortified.

"So," Amara said, the laughter gone, replaced by a sharp, business-like focus. "Since we have both resigned from the culture war... and since our spouses are currently tracking our locations via 'Find My Friends'... what are we doing, Darius?"

Darius looked at the Scrabble board. *QUIET. TRAUMA. EXIT.*

He looked at the window. He imagined the world out there—the noise, the demands, the relentless performance of being a Good Black Citizen and a Good Spouse.

"We are forming a union," he said.

Amara raised an eyebrow. "A union?"

"Collective bargaining," Darius said. The tech executive part of his brain—the part that understood leverage and systems—was waking up. "Individually, we are weak. If I go back to Atlanta now, I'll just slide back into the routine. I'll be the Prop within 24 hours. If you go back to Portland, you'll just start editing college essays and soothing Carter's tax anxiety."

"True," she murmured. "I'm already pre-exhausted just thinking about it."

"But here," Darius said, gesturing to the small, damp room. "Here, we have leverage. We are... witnesses."

"Witnesses to what?"

"To the fact that we exist," he said. "That we are people. Not props. Not utilities. Not symbols of resilience. Just... people who like bad wine and silence."

Amara stared at him. She was processing it. He could see the gears turning—the intellect that had gotten her a Ph.D. dismantling his argument, checking for structural weaknesses, and finding none.

"So," she said slowly. "A Non-Aggression Pact."

"Exactly. A treaty."

"What are the terms?"

Darius leaned forward. He pushed the Scrabble board aside. This was the real game now.

"Rule One," he said. "No sex. That complicates the audit. We are not here to blow up our lives; we are here to survive them. If we sleep together, it becomes a soap opera. If we don't, it's a strategy."

Amara nodded. "Agreed. I have enough laundry to do at home; I don't need the emotional laundry of an affair. Plus, sex requires cardio, and I'm on sabbatical. It doesn't mean I don't want it though. Mistakes will happen," she coyly says.

"Rule Two," Darius continued. "No trauma dumping. I don't want to hear about your childhood, and you don't want to hear about my mother. We deal with the 'now.' We deal with the weather, the Scrabble score, and the food. We are not each other's therapists."

"Thank God," Amara said. "I charge $250 an hour, and you can't afford me."

"Rule Three," Darius said. "Total honesty. If you're boring me, I will tell you. If I'm chewing too loud, you tell me. No politeness. No

'Southern Hospitality.' No 'British Stiff Upper Lip.' I'm sick of being polite."

"Done," Amara said. "If you play another two-letter word in Scrabble, I will flip the table. That's my honesty."

"And Rule Four," she added, picking up her wine glass and swirling the last drops. "We don't talk about the news. The White, Black, Asian, Latino, Trans folks got it. We are strictly observers. If the world ends, we watch it from the porch."

Darius felt a weight lift off his chest—a physical sensation, like a heavy backpack being unbuckled and dropped to the floor.

"Rule Four is the most important one," he said.

He held out his hand. "We protect each other."

Amara looked at it. Her hand was small, strong, and stained with a bit of ink from the crossword puzzle she had done earlier.

She took his hand. Her grip was firm. It wasn't the soft, tentative shake of a social introduction. It was the grip of a co-conspirator.

"Deal," she said.

"Deal."

They didn't let go immediately. For three seconds, they just held the connection—a handshake that felt more intimate than a kiss because it was based on a contract, not a fantasy. It was an acknowledgement that they were both AWOL from the same war.

Then Amara pulled her hand back. She picked up a tile from the velvet bag.

"Your turn," she said. "And if you play 'V-I-B-E,' I'm evicting you."

Darius looked at his rack. He smiled.

He placed his tiles.

E-X-I-T.

"Fourteen points," he said.

"Acceptable," Amara said.

Outside, the rain hammered against the roof, sealing them in. But for the first time in years, the noise didn't bother Darius.

He wasn't a prop. He wasn't a soldier. He was a shareholder.

And the meeting had just begun.

CHAPTER 10: THE BREACH
(THE AUDIT)

Part I: The Anniversary

T he one-year anniversary of the first retreat arrived the way most sacred things do in the lives of overworked Black adults—quietly, without fanfare, without permission, and without the world knowing it was a holy day.

They didn't plan it on a shared Google Calendar. They didn't send an invite. They didn't acknowledge it with a card or a gift.

They just arrived.

They rented two cottages again—Cabin One and Cabin Two— because ritual mattered. Structure mattered. Plausible deniability was the rent they paid for their peace.

But they only lived in one.

Cabin One stood cold and empty on the ridge, holding nothing but Amara's easel, a half-finished canvas dominated by chaotic, violent blues, and a ceramic mug she always forgot on the porch railing. It was a decoy. A shell company for her soul.

Cabin Two held everything else. It held their bags. It held the smell of Darius's sandalwood soap and Amara's mint tea. It held their laughter, which had softened from the desperate, hysterical release of the first trip into a low, steady hum.

The lake was a sheet of hammered silver that evening, motionless under a sky that looked like a fresh bruise—purple, gray, and heavy with unshed rain. The air outside smelled of cedar smoke and cold water, the kind of scent that clears your sinuses and sharpens your edges.

Inside Cabin Two, the fire crackled in the stone hearth, throwing warm, dancing light across the high timber beams. The heat made the windows fog at the edges, sealing them inside a snow globe of their own making.

The air inside was thick, intimate, and smelled of burning wood and the faint, medicinal tang of eucalyptus.

Dung-chul—the Golden Retriever was currently on a union-mandated break from his guard duties—was asleep on the rug. He snored softly, his paws twitching in a rhythmic dance, chasing squirrels through a dreamscape where he was always fast enough.

Amara sat cross-legged on the floor.

She wasn't wearing the "armor" of Dr. Lewis—no blazer, no heels, no empathetic nod. She was wearing gray sweatpants that were slightly too long and an oversized hoodie that swallowed her hands. Her hair was tied up in a messy knot that defied gravity and logic.

On her face, a green clay mask had dried into a cracked mosaic. She couldn't smile without breaking the crust, so she didn't. She looked like a swamp creature who had found enlightenment.

She looked like a woman who had finally stopped performing.

Darius sat opposite her, leaning back against the leather couch, a heavy wool blanket draped over his legs. He wasn't coding. He wasn't managing. He wasn't fixing a filter, a server, or a crisis.

He was holding a Scrabble tile tray as if it were a weapon of war.

"Qi is a word," he insisted, his voice low and gravelly, vibrating with the seriousness of a man defending his honor.

"It's a cheap word," Amara countered, not looking up from her own letters. Her voice was muffled slightly by the mask. "It's a word for people who have given up on vowels. It's lazy, Darius."

"It's strategic. It's ten points. Plus the triple letter score."

"It's spiritual bypassing," she said, finally looking at him. Her eyes crinkled, cracking the green clay at her temples. "You're using life force energy to score points. It's tacky."

"It's in the dictionary, Amara. The official Scrabble dictionary. Are you arguing with Merriam-Webster?"

"I'm arguing with your soul."

Dung-chul snorted in his sleep, a long, rattling sound that seemed to side with the prosecution.

The wind outside rattled the heavy timber frames of the windows, a reminder of the cold world they had locked out. But in here, the fire popped, sending a tiny ember skittering across the grate.

It was peaceful. It was boring. It was the most dangerous room on earth.

Darius leaned back against the counter, blowing steam off his mug. He looked at the digital clock on the microwave, then at the darkened screen of his phone on the table.

"You know what I haven't thought about in seventy-two hours?" he asked.

"Your cholesterol?"

"The Executive Branch," Darius said. "I haven't thought about the White House, the Senate, or the price of eggs and bread. I haven't watched a single press conference where a geriatric man shouts at a cloud, or a press secretary tries to explain why 'up' actually means 'down' in this economy."

Amara laughed, stirring a spoonful of raw sugar into her cup. "It's been peaceful. The Empire is crumbling, Rome is burning, and we're just here... exfoliating."

"It's not just the crumbling," Darius said, shaking his head. "It's the *volume* of the crumbling. The last few years? It's been like being trapped in a writer's room where everyone is high, and nobody has an editor. First, we had the Reality Show season. Then we had the Nursing Home season. Now? I don't even know what genre we're in. Is it a tragedy? A sitcom? A documentary on institutional decline?"

"It's a farce," Amara said. "With a high budget."

She took a sip of coffee. "I stopped watching. That was my resolution last year. I realized that my blood pressure was directly tied to the C-SPAN chyron. I told Carter, 'I am retiring from the Department of Caring About Foolishness.' He didn't understand. He wanted to discuss the geopolitical implications of the latest scandal. I told him, 'Unless the scandal is in my bank account or my backyard, I am unavailable for comment."

"That's the secret," Darius said, pointing a finger at her. "That is the doctrine. The world wants us to be outraged. It needs our outrage. It runs on Black cortisol. If we aren't marching, or tweeting, or stressing over which old white man is going to ruin the interest rates, the machine breaks."

"I resigned," Amara said, raising her hand as if swearing an oath. "I sent my letter of resignation to the Republic. I said, 'Dear America, good luck with that. I have a hydrafacial at three."

Darius chuckled, a deep, rich sound. "I saw a headline right before the storm hit. Some bill they were trying to pass. Something about 'reclaiming heritage.' I started to read it, and then I felt my chest get tight. And I asked myself: 'Darius, will reading this change the law? No. Will it make you want to punch a wall? Yes.' So I closed the tab. I put the phone down. I minded my Black ass business."

"And the sun still rose," Amara whispered.

"The sun still rose," Darius confirmed. "And the coffee is still hot. And the fools in D.C. are still fools, regardless of whether I witness their foolishness."

He looked at her, his expression turning serious, almost reverent.

"That's the luxury, Amara. They sold us on the idea that being 'informed' was a duty. But for people like us? Ignorance isn't bliss. It's self-preservation. Minding your business isn't a lack of patriotism. It's a health plan."

"It's a spiritual practice," Amara agreed, clinking her mug against his. "To the Republic."

"To the Republic," Darius said. "May it figure its own shit out, because I am off the clock."

Part II: The Glitch

Atlanta. Four hours earlier.

Sasha had been watching Darius for months.

She watched him not with the paranoid frenzy of a jealous wife, but with the cold, clinical precision of a scientist studying a glitch in the data.

She tracked the variables.

The humming. He never hummed before. Now, he hummed as he worked. He hummed while folding laundry. He hummed Coltrane, a sound that vibrated in his chest, making the kitchen feel smaller.

The smiling. Not the camera-ready smile he used for her stories, the one that showed teeth but no eyes. This was a private smile. A smile he tucked into the corner of his mouth when he looked at his phone, or out the window, or at nothing at all.

The softness. His shoulders had dropped two inches. The tension that used to vibrate off him—the "Prop" energy—was gone. He sat down without being asked. He breathed like someone who had discovered oxygen for the first time.

She had checked the usual suspects.

She sniffed his shirts when he threw them in the hamper. Nothing but his own detergent. No perfume. No hotel soap. No unfamiliar shampoo.

She checked his mileage. Normal. Commutes to the office (when he goes), runs to the grocery store, and the occasional drive to the hardware store.

She checked his credit card statements. Groceries. Gas. A new hard drive.

There were no receipts for jewelry. No dinners for two at the places she liked. No hotel charges.

But the happiness—that was the evidence.

Happiness was a foreign contaminant in their marriage. It hadn't been introduced by her, which meant it was being imported.

And Darius, in his newfound ease, had gotten sloppy. Ease makes you drop your guard. Ease makes you forget that you live in a panopticon.

The man who built encrypted servers in his basement and lectured the twins on digital hygiene had forgotten to disable the "Find My" location on the iPad he packed in his duffel bag.

He had packed it because he wanted to read a specific out-of-print sci-fi novel on the flight. He hadn't turned it on. But the background refresh was active.

Sasha sat in her car in the driveway of their Buckhead home, the engine idling. She stared at her phone.

The dot pulsed.

It wasn't in Seattle. It wasn't at a conference center.

It was on the Olympic Peninsula.

She zoomed in. There were no hotels. There were no tech summits. There was just a jagged coastline, a dense green void of forest, and a single road that ended at a cluster of cabins.

Sasha felt a coldness spread through her chest. It wasn't heartbreak. Heartbreak required vulnerability. This was rage. This was the icy fury of a project manager realizing someone had messed with the spreadsheet.

She didn't cry. She didn't call her sister. She didn't post a cryptic quote on her story.

She put the car in reverse.

She didn't pack a bag. She didn't need clothes. She wasn't staying. She was going to fly to whereever he is and see what is happening. She was going to burn it down, and then she was coming home.

Part III: The Drive

The drive from the airport to the peninsula was a descent into madness.

The rental car was a cheap sedan that smelled of stale cigarettes and pine air freshener—a mockery of the real pine passing in a blur outside.

Rain streaked across the windshield, blurring the towering trees into dark, looming ghosts. The wipers thumped in a steady, irritated rhythm. *Thump-thump. Thump-thump.*

Sasha gripped the steering wheel so hard her manicure dug into the leather.

Her mind played a movie on loop, a high-definition 4K horror film.

Darius in bed with a woman. A younger woman. A woman who looked at him with big, adoring eyes and didn't ask him to fix the WiFi.

Darius tangled in sheets that weren't Egyptian cotton. Darius betraying her with sweat and skin and moans she hadn't heard in a decade.

She rehearsed the confrontation. She directed the scene.

She would burst in. He would be naked. He would scramble to cover himself, looking pathetic and small. The woman would scream. Sasha would stand there, impeccable in her trench coat, and deliver the line that would end him.

I hope she was worth half your assets.

Or maybe: *Get dressed. You look ridiculous.*

She refined the dialogue. She adjusted the lighting in her mind. She needed him to be pathetic. She needed him to be wrong. Because if he was wrong, she was right. And Sasha needed to be right more than she needed to be happy. The wipers slashed across the windshield of the car, fighting a losing battle against the deluge. Sasha's knuckles were white on the leather steering wheel. The GPS promised arrival in some minutes, but her panic demanded it be five. She picks up the phone to call her sister Niecy.

It rang twice before her sister picked up. The background noise was loud—kids screaming, a TV blaring cartoons.

"What?" Niecy answered. No hello. Just the exhaustion of a Saturday afternoon.

"I found him," Sasha said, her voice trembling with a mix of adrenaline and rage. "Niecy, I found him. He's at a cabin. In the middle of nowhere. And he's not alone. I know he's not."

She waited for the gasp. She waited for the rallying cry, for Niecy to say, *"Oh, hell no. Turn the car around, pick me up, and let's go burn it down."*

Instead, there was a long pause. Then the sound of a door closing, muting the cartoon noise.

"Okay," Niecy said. Her voice was disturbingly calm. "And what are you going to do when you get there?"

"What am I going to do?" Sasha shrieked, nearly swerving into the shoulder. "I'm going to catch him! He's cheating, Niecy! Darius—Mr. Perfect, Mr. Reliable, Mr. 'I'm working late on the server migration'—is shacking up with some... some bitch in the woods!"

"Maybe," Niecy said.

"Maybe? What do you mean, maybe?"

"I mean, maybe he is," Niecy said, her voice flat. "And if he is... I'm surprised it took him this long."

Sasha slammed on the brakes as a deer darted across the road. The car skidded slightly on the wet asphalt before the traction control kicked in. She gasped, her heart hammering against her ribs.

"Excuse me?" Sasha whispered. "Whose side are you on?"

"I'm on the side of reality, Sasha," Niecy sighed. "Look, I love you. You're my sister. I will help you bury a body if I have to. But I am not going to sit here and act shocked that Darius finally snapped."

"I give that man everything!" Sasha yelled at the dashboard. "I run his house. I raise his kids. I manage his life!"

"You manage your *brand*, baby," Niecy corrected sharply. "You don't manage his life. You manage the lighting. You manage the aesthetic. I've been over there for dinner, Sasha. You talk to that man like he's a staff member. 'Darius, move the car.' 'Darius, hold the camera.' 'Darius, sign the check.' The man is an ATM that breathes. He runs that house and you are a tool."

"He likes it!" Sasha protested, tears stinging her eyes. "He likes being useful!"

"Nobody likes being used, Sasha. They just tolerate it until they don't."

"Oh, really?" Sasha let out a bitter, jagged laugh. "If you think he's such a victim, why do you always have your hand out? 'Niecy needs braces for the kids.' 'Niecy's transmission blew.' You don't have a problem treating him like an ATM when you need five hundred dollars!"

The silence on the line was heavy. It stretched for three seconds, thick with the truth.

"You're right," Niecy said softly. "I do ask. And you know why? Because he never says no. He writes the check, he fixes the car, and he never looks at me like I'm a charity case. He's a good man, Sasha. He is a decent, heavy-lifting man."

Niecy took a breath. "But I'm his sister-in-law. I'm supposed to be annoying. You're his *wife*. You're supposed to be his peace. And be honest with me right now—when was the last time you looked at Darius and saw anything other than a prop for your social media story?"

Sasha opened her mouth, but the words died in her throat. She saw the road stretching out before her. She saw the last ten years. She saw the tripod. She saw the ring light. She couldn't remember the last time she saw *him*.

"I didn't think he had it in him," Niecy said, her voice quiet now, almost admiring. "I really didn't. I thought he'd just keep his head down and pay the bills until he died of a heart attack at fifty. All I ask is that you hear him out and don't assume yet."

"So what are you saying?" Sasha whispered, wiping a tear from her cheek.

"I'm saying," Niecy replied, "that if Darius found a way to breathe for a minute... good for him. And them kids, they are some trolls, and you know it. They don't know the meaning of respect or hard work. They look down on me."

"Good for him?" Sasha screamed. "He is destroying our family!"

"Maybe," Niecy said. "Or maybe he's just trying to survive it."

Click.

The line went dead. Sasha stared at the screen, the car's silence deafening against the roar of the rain. She threw the phone onto the passenger seat.

"Good for him," she muttered, gripping the wheel until her fingers ached. "We'll see about that."

She slammed her foot on the gas. The cabin was two miles away.

The GPS chirped. *Destination on the left.*

She turned onto the gravel road. The stones crunched under her tires—a violent, popping sound in the quiet forest.

She saw the cabin. It was dark, angular, hidden in the trees. It looked like a bunker.

She saw the rental car in the driveway. A sensible SUV.

She parked behind it, blocking it in. A tactical move. No escape.

She got out. The rain hit her face, cold and shocking. It ruined her blowout in seconds. She didn't care.

She marched toward the door, phone in hand, the tracking dot pulsing like a second heartbeat.

She didn't knock.

She didn't pause to listen.

She didn't breathe.

She grabbed the handle. It was unlocked. Of course it was unlocked. He felt safe.

She threw the door open.

Part IV: The Breach

The violence of her entry was immediate.

The wind rushed in with her, a cold, wet vortex that swirled through the warm, cedar-scented air of the cabin. The heavy door banged hard against the interior wall—*WHAM*—shaking the frame.

Leaves skittered across the floorboards.

Sasha stood in the doorway, chest heaving, hair plastered to her cheeks, eyes wild and hunting, hoping to see some skin.

"Surprise," she hissed, the word tearing out of her throat.

And then she froze.

The movie in her head stopped. The film reel burned.

Darius and Amara looked up at her from the floor.

Not from a bed. Not from a tangle of sweaty limbs. Not from a compromising position that she could screenshot and send to a lawyer.

From a Scrabble board.

Darius held a tile in mid-air, his hand suspended halfway to the board. He looked at his wife standing in the doorway, dripping wet and vibrating with rage.

He didn't flinch. He didn't scramble to cover himself with a pillow. He didn't jump up and stammer an excuse.

He didn't look pale or guilty or terrified.

He looked... annoyed.

He looked like a man who was reading a very good book and had just been interrupted by a door-to-door salesman.

He lowered the tile slowly to the board. *Click.*

He took a sip of his tea while Sasha closed the door.

He pulled the wool blanket slightly higher on his chest, not to hide his body, but because the door was opened and she let the heat out.

Dung-chul lifted his heavy head from the rug. He looked at the wet woman in the doorway, barked once—a short, sharp sound of disapproval at the draft—and then flopped back down when Amara looked at him.

Sasha stepped fully into the room. Water pooled around her expensive boots.

Her eyes scanned the room, desperate for the sin. She needed the sin.

She looked for a bed unmade, rumpled, but there was nothing. One book on the nightstand.

She looked at the dining table. Two mugs. A plate of half-eaten crackers. A bag of beef jerky.

She looked at the woman.

Amara sat on the floor, legs crossed in a pretzel. She was wearing gray sweatpants that had seen better days and a hoodie that looked like it belonged to a giant.

And on her face... green mud.

A face mask. Cracking. Dry.

She wasn't wearing lingerie. She wasn't wearing makeup. She was wearing thick, gray wool socks.

Sasha's brain stuttered. It couldn't process the image. The data didn't match the query.

This wasn't an affair scene. This wasn't sex. This wasn't passion.

This was... domesticity.

This was... gentle.

This was... happy.

It hit Sasha harder than any sexual betrayal could have. It felt like a physical blow to the sternum, knocking the wind out of her.

He isn't cheating on me with sex, she realized, the thought landing with the weight of a stone. *He's cheating on me with peace.*

The silence stretched. It was agonizing. The only sound was the wind hissing through the open door and the soft crackle of the fire.

Sasha stood there, vibrating, waiting for the apology. Waiting for Darius to realize the magnitude of his error, to fall to his knees, to beg.

But he didn't. He just sat there, warm and unbothered, watching her drip on the floorboards.

Amara sighed.

It was a long, loud, weary exhale. The sound of a mechanic looking at a transmission that had blown out at 4:55 PM on a Friday.

She placed her remaining letters face down on the board. She unfolded her legs and stood up.

She didn't rush. She didn't adjust her clothes to look more presentable. She didn't touch her face mask to hide the cracks.

She moved with the slow, deliberate energy of a woman who was strictly off the clock.

"Well," Amara said. Her voice was calm, crisp, and accented. She dusted cracker crumbs off her sweatpants.

"Looks like y'all have some shit to talk about."

Sasha stared at her, her mouth falling open. The casual profanity, delivered in that polished British tone, was like a slap.

"Excuse me?" Sasha whispered.

Amara didn't answer. She walked over to the coffee table and picked up a set of keys and the raincoat. Snapping her fingers to Dung-Chul, who was watching Sasha like a sniper.

The keys jangled loudly in the quiet room. The wooden fob was large and engraved: **CABIN 1**.

"I'm going to my cabin," Amara said, casually gesturing toward the door, toward the dark, rain-soaked woods outside. "I was just leaving anyway. Darius was cheating."

Sasha flinched. The word hung in the air.

"At Scrabble," Amara clarified dryly.

She walked toward the door. She had to pass within inches of Sasha to get out.

Sasha braced herself. She expected the woman to shrink. To skirt around her. To look down in shame.

Amara didn't shrink. She didn't apologize. She didn't even speed up.

She walked past Sasha with a breezy confidence, smelling of peppermint and expensive clay.

She paused at the threshold, holding the door handle. She looked back at the frozen tableau—Darius sitting comfortably under his blanket, sipping his tea; Sasha standing like a storm cloud in the center of the room.

"There's tea on the stove," Amara said, pointing to the kettle with her keys. Her eyes met Sasha's, and for a second, Sasha saw not fear, but a profound, exhausting pity.

"Ginger and turmeric. It's good for the nerves."

She stepped out into the rain.

She pulled the door shut behind her with a soft, decisive *click*.

Sasha stood there, shaking with rage, staring at the closed door.

She looked at the tea kettle.

She looked at her husband, who was calmly arranging his letters on the rack, sliding the tiles around with a soft *clack-clack-clack*, as if waiting for her to stop dripping so he could take his turn.

She has her own cabin?

She's wearing a face mask?

She just offered me ginger?

Sasha unclenched her jaw just enough to force the words out through her teeth.

"This bitch."

Part V: The Fallout (The Audit)

The door clicked shut, sealing them in.

The room, which moments ago had felt like a sanctuary, instantly curdled. The warmth of the fire seemed to evaporate, replaced by the cold radiation of Sasha's presence.

Sasha didn't leave the spot by the door. She stood there, water pooling around her boots, seeping into the vintage rug. She was trembling—not just shivering from the rain, but vibrating with a frequency that felt like it could shatter glass.

She stared at the closed door for a long time, as if she could burn a hole through it with her eyes and incinerate the woman on the other side.

Then, slowly, mechanically, she turned her head to look at her husband.

She looked like a predator who had just watched a gazelle trot away unharmed and was now turning its attention to the slow, injured thing left behind.

"So," Sasha said. Her voice was unrecognizable. It was thin, stripped of its usual polish. "That's the play? She just... leaves? And I'm supposed to believe she's going to her 'own cabin'?"

Darius took a sip of his tea. His hand was steady, though his heart was hammering a frantic rhythm against his ribs. He knew the physics of this moment. If he showed fear, she would pounce. If he showed guilt, she would win. If he apologized, he would lose the ground he had spent a year building.

"She has the key, Sasha," Darius said calmly. "You saw the fob."

"I saw a prop!" Sasha snapped. The volume of her voice made the dog flinch in his sleep.

She marched over to the bedroom door. She ripped the duvet off the bed, shaking it violently, looking for what? A hidden lover? A second pillow?

She checked the sheets. One scent. His.

She opened the closet door and shoved his flannel shirts aside, the hangers clattering together like bones. She was looking for the silk. The lace. The evidence of the fantasy she had built in her car.

Darius watched her. He didn't move. He didn't offer an explanation. He let her audit the room. He let her realize that the only ghost in here was her own insecurity.

She marched into the bathroom. He heard the medicine cabinet open and slam shut. *Bang.*

He heard the shower curtain rip back. *Swish.*

She came back into the living room, empty-handed. She was breathing hard, her chest heaving under her soaked coat. Her eyes were wild, darting around the room, desperate for a target.

"Where is it?" she demanded.

"Where is what?"

"The stuff, Darius! The toothbrush. The night cream. The earrings on the nightstand. Where did she hide it?"

"She didn't hide it," Darius said. "She has it with her. To Cabin One. Because that's where she sleeps. We are neighbors."

Sasha stared at him. The logic was impenetrable, and it infuriated her. She walked over to the Scrabble board. She looked at the tiles.

She looked at the scorecard on the notepad. *Amara: 142. Darius: 108.*

Sasha swiped the tile rack off the table.

It clattered onto the floor, wooden letters scattering like teeth across the hardwood. *A. E. R. T. Q.*

"Don't you dare," she hissed, pointing a manicured finger at his face. "Don't you dare sit there wrapped in a blanket and gaslight me. You are sleeping with her."

"No," Darius said.

"You are in love with her."

Darius paused.

The silence stretched, thin and tight as a piano wire. He looked at his wife—really looked at her. He saw the wet hair plastered to her skull. He saw the mascara smudged under her left eye. He saw the terrified child hiding behind the angry woman.

He realized he didn't have the energy to lie anymore.

"I am peaceful with her," he said.

Sasha recoiled as if he had slapped her. She physically stumbled back a step, her hand flying to her chest.

"That is worse," she whispered, her voice breaking. "Do you understand that? That is worse!"

She began to pace, her wet boots squeaking on the wood. *Squeak. Step. Squeak.*

"You think you're so deep," she spat, gesturing wildly. "You think you're some tortured artist who needs 'peace.' You're a cliché, Darius. You're a middle-aged man having a crisis because real life is too hard, so you ran away to play house in the woods."

"She asks me to be myself," Darius said quietly.

"Yourself?" Sasha laughed, a harsh, barking sound that had no humor in it. "Darius, without me, 'yourself' is a guy in a basement coding toys. I built you. I polished you. I made you palatable to the world."

"I didn't ask to be palatable," Darius said. "I asked to be known by my family."

Sasha stopped pacing. She looked at the empty spot where Amara had been sitting. She looked at the half-empty mug of tea.

And suddenly, the rage fractured into something sharper, something far more humiliated.

"Are you serious?" she muttered, more to herself than to him. "She's… she's fucking beautiful."

Darius blinked. "Sasha—"

"No, don't 'Sasha' me," she snapped, pacing a tight circle, her hands flying up to her hair. "She's beautiful with her English ass. And that accent? That accent is a weapon. I stood there listening to her offer me tea, and I didn't know if I was supposed to beat her ass or offer her a biscuit."

Her voice cracked on the last word, spiraling into a manic, high-pitched laugh.

"She's pretty. She's calm. She's got that face mask on like she's in a spa commercial. And she's sitting on the floor playing Scrabble like she's not a threat."

She turned to Darius, eyes wide, tears finally spilling over.

"Do you know what that does to a woman? To walk in and see someone that pretty, that peaceful, that unbothered... in *your* peace or being your peace?"

She let out a shaky breath, wrapping her arms around her wet coat.

"It messes with your mind, Darius. It makes me feel like I'm the noise."

Darius looked at her. He didn't deny it. He couldn't.

"You could've told me," she whispered.

"I did," Darius said. "For years. I told you I was tired. I told you I felt like an ATM. I told you I needed to stop performing."

She opened her mouth—then closed it.

"I didn't know you were unhappy," she whispered.

"I wasn't unhappy," Darius said. "I was hollow."

"That's the same thing."

"No," he said gently. "It's not. Unhappy is a feeling. Hollow is a condition."

Sasha's voice cracked. "So what... I'm the reason you're hollow?"

"You're part of the excavation," Darius said. "I am never your first option."

The honesty was a knife. Sasha staggered back a step, as if the air had punched her. She looked at the fire, desperate for something to focus on besides the ruin of her marriage.

"I didn't ask you to disappear into yourself," she said weakly.

"No," Darius said. "You just didn't notice when I did."

The silence that followed was suffocating. The fire popped.

Sasha's voice dropped to a whisper. She looked at the floor, at the scattered tiles.

"Do you want to be with her?"

"No."

"Do you want to be with me?"

Darius didn't answer immediately.

He looked at the fire. He looked at the blanket over his legs. He felt the phantom weight of Amara's hand in his from earlier that day.

Then he looked at his wife.

"I want to be with myself," he said.

Sasha's breath caught.

"And I don't know if I can do that with you," he added. "I don't know if you have room for me. The real me. Not the Prop. I am always the last in line with your family."

The room tilted. Sasha felt something inside her collapse— quietly, like a shelf giving way under too much weight.

She took a shaky breath. She wiped her face, smearing mascara across her cheek. She looked small.

"So what happens now?"

Darius leaned back against the couch. He looked exhausted, but lighter than he had in years.

"We talk," he said. "We figure out what this is. What it isn't. What it can be."

Sasha sniffed. "And if I don't like the answers?"

"Then we make new ones," Darius said. "Or we stop pretending."

Sasha looked around the room again—the fire, the blanket, the peace. She looked at her husband, who suddenly felt like a stranger even though she doesn't know him. A man she had never bothered to meet because she was too busy managing her image of him.

She whispered, "I don't know how to do this. I don't know how to just... be."

"I know," Darius said softly. "But we're going to have to try."

Sasha nodded slowly, her throat tight.

She wasn't ready. She wasn't steady. She wasn't okay.

But she wasn't leaving. Not yet. The rain was too hard, and the truth was too cold.

She walked to the armchair across from him—the one Amara hadn't used—and sat down, dripping water onto the rug. She pulled her coat tighter.

"Okay," she said quietly. "Talk."

Darius took a breath—a long, steady inhale that filled his chest with cedar and smoke.

And the conversation that would change everything began.

CHAPTER 11: THE FALLOUT (THE AUDIT)

Part I: The Anchor (Amara's Cabin)

The walk back to Cabin One was wet, dark, and utterly devoid of drama.

In a movie, this would be the scene where the mistress runs through the woods sobbing, tripping over roots, terrified of the retribution coming for her. She would be clutching her chest, wondering if she had just destroyed a family.

Amara walked at a steady, leisurely pace.

She didn't run. She didn't look back. She used the flashlight on her phone and Dung-Chul to illuminate the path, stepping carefully over the slick roots, not because she was fleeing, but because she didn't want to muddy her favorite wool socks.

She reached the porch of Cabin One. It was dark, save for the amber glow of the motion-sensor light that clicked on to greet her.

She keyed in the code.

The door unlocked with a heavy, satisfying thunk.

She stepped inside. The air here was different from that in Cabin Two. It was cooler, smelling of turpentine, dried acrylics, and the lavender laundry detergent she used for her throws. It smelled like *her*.

She locked the door behind her. She didn't deadbolt it out of fear; she deadbolted it out of habit. The world stayed out. The peace stayed in.

She slipped off her wet boots and lined them up on the mat.

She walked to the kitchenette and filled the electric kettle. She didn't shake. Her hands were steady as she spooned loose-leaf Earl Grey into the strainer.

While the water heated, she walked to the large easel set up by the window.

The canvas was dominated by a violent, swirling blue—the color of the lake during the storm two years ago. It wasn't finished. The edges were still raw, the composition unbalanced.

She picked up a palette knife.

She didn't think about Sasha screaming in Cabin Two. She didn't worry about Darius.

She knew Darius. She knew the geography of his patience. She knew that right now, he wasn't cowering under Sasha's rage; he was likely sitting in that leather chair, wrapped in his blanket, watching his wife's anger burn itself out like a grease fire.

He didn't need Amara to save him. He didn't need her to intervene. He just needed her to hold the line.

Click. The kettle boiled.

Amara poured the water. The steam rose, curling around her face.

She took the mug to the window seat—a deep, cushioned alcove that looked out toward the woods separating the two cabins. She couldn't see Cabin Two from here, just the wall of black pines and the driving rain.

She took a sip of tea. It was hot, bergamot-heavy, grounding.

She thought about Sasha's face in the doorway. The shock. The confusion. The way she had looked at Amara was not as a monster, but as a mirror.

Amara didn't feel smug. She didn't feel triumphant.

She felt a profound, heavy sadness for the woman standing in the rain.

"She doesn't know," Amara whispered to the empty room.

Sasha didn't know that the enemy wasn't the woman in the sweatpants. The enemy was the silence she had never learned to befriend. Sasha thought she was fighting for her husband, but she was actually fighting for her reflection.

Amara pulled her legs up, tucking her knees under her chin.

She opened her book—*The Body Keeps the Score*—to the page she had marked.

She read the same paragraph three times, but her mind drifted back to the Scrabble board. She smiled.

She had been winning. *Qi*. Ten points. Triple letter score.

She wondered if Sasha had flipped the board. Probably. Sasha was a flipper. Darius was a stacker.

Amara turned the page.

She wasn't waiting for a text. She wasn't waiting for him to come knocking on her door in the rain, breathless and apologetic.

They had built the Union for this exact moment. They had built it to withstand the audit.

She took another sip of tea, the ceramic warming her hands.

"You've got this, Darius," she murmured softly, her voice calm in the quiet cabin.

She turned on the small reading lamp, casting a warm circle of light against the dark glass. She wasn't hiding. She was simply, unapologetically, waiting for the noise to stop.

Because the noise always stopped eventually. But the Union? The Union was structural.

Amara turned the page, and in the silence of Cabin One, she kept reading. A soft shuffle broke the silence.

Dung-chul padded out from the shadowed hallway, nails clicking lightly against the wood. He didn't bark or whine. He simply walked over and sat beside her chair, pressing his warm body against her calf like he was plugging her back into the earth.

Amara exhaled, the breath leaving her in a slow, trembling ribbon she hadn't realized she was holding.

"I'm fine," she whispered, though she wasn't sure if she meant it for herself or for him.

Dung-chul rested his chin on her knee, heavy and certain. The kind of weight that didn't ask anything of her. The kind that said *I'm here. Stay right here.*

Her hand drifted down, fingers sliding into the thick fur at his neck. He didn't move. Didn't demand. Just stayed.

The lamp hummed softly. The tea cooled. The world outside remained dark and indifferent.

But Dung-chul stayed pressed against her leg, steady as a heartbeat.

And for the first time that day, Amara felt something unclench — small, but real.

She turned another page. Dung-chul sighed and settled in closer.

Silence, finally, felt like company.

Part II: The Retreat (Sasha's Exit)

Sasha nodded slowly, her throat tight.

She wasn't ready to try. Not tonight. The air in the cabin was too thin for her. It was too honest. She felt like she was hyperventilating on pure oxygen.

"I can't stay here," she whispered.

Darius didn't argue. He didn't offer her the spare room. He didn't offer her tea.

"Okay," he said.

Sasha pulled her coat tighter. The wet wool was heavy, dragging her down. She walked to the door, her boots squelching on the rug.

She paused with her hand on the latch. She looked back at him one last time.

She wanted to say something devastating. She wanted to say something that would make him hurt the way she was hurting.

But all she could think of was the way he looked at the Scrabble board.

"You were winning," she said, her voice hollow.

"No," Darius said gently. "She was beating me by forty points."

Sasha swallowed. She opened the door. The wind rushed in again, cold and unforgiving.

"Goodbye, Darius," she said.

She stepped out into the night and pulled the door shut.

The walk to the car was a blur. The rain had picked up again, slashing sideways. She stumbled on a root, catching herself on the hood of the car.

She wrenched the door open and climbed inside.

She locked the doors. *Click.*

She sat there in the dark, the engine off, listening to the rain drum against the roof. It was deafening.

She reached for her phone. Her thumb hovered over her other sister's contact. *Maya.*

Maya would validate her. Maya would tell her Darius was having a midlife crisis. Maya would tell her to call a lawyer, freeze the accounts, and burn the cabin down.

Sasha stared at the name.

She realized, with a sinking horror, that she didn't want validation. She didn't want the script.

If she told Maya, it became real. If she told Maya, it became content. *The Betrayal. The Divorce Arc.*

Sasha put the phone down in the cup holder. She didn't call.

She put her hands on the steering wheel. She stared into the black woods where Amara's cabin was hidden.

For the first time in her life, Sasha sat in the silence.

And she screamed.

It wasn't a content-creator scream. It wasn't pretty. It was a guttural, animal sound that tore her throat raw. She screamed until her lungs burned, until the windows fogged up with her rage.

Then, she started the car. She put it in reverse.

She backed out of the driveway, her headlights sweeping over the cabin one last time. She saw the glow of the fire in the window.

She turned the car around and drove into the dark, leaving the peace behind to drive straight to the airport.

Part III: The Aftermath

Inside Cabin Two, the silence returned.

But it was different now. It was bruised.

Darius sat on the couch for a long time after the sound of Sasha's engine faded down the road.

He didn't move. He didn't drink his tea. He just listened to the fire popping.

His hands were shaking. Just a little. A fine tremor in his fingers.

The adrenaline was leaving his body, and in its wake, he felt an exhaustion so profound it felt like gravity had doubled.

He looked at the puddle of water Sasha had left on the floor. It was already seeping into the wood, darkening the grain.

He stood up. His knees cracked.

He walked to the kitchen and got a towel. He got down on his hands and knees and wiped up the water.

He scrubbed the floor until the wood was dry. It felt like penance. It felt like prayer.

Then, he walked to the Scrabble board.

He picked up the tile rack Sasha had thrown. He found the scattered letters under the table, near the dog's paws, by the fireplace.

A. E. R. T. Q.

He placed them back in the velvet bag. He folded the board.

He looked at the empty mug of turmeric tea Amara had left.

He picked it up. He walked to the kitchen sink and rinsed it out.

He stood at the sink, looking out the window into the darkness. He couldn't see Cabin One from here, but he knew she was there.

He knew she was probably painting. Or reading. Or just sitting in the dark, waiting for the signal that the storm had passed.

Darius leaned his forehead against the cold glass.

He had blown up his life. He had told the truth. He had stripped the wires.

He felt lighter than air.

He went to the turntable. The record had finished ages ago, the needle sitting in the run-out groove, a soft *thump-thump-thump* like a heartbeat.

He lifted the arm. He flipped the record.

He dropped the needle.

Bill Evans. *Peace Piece.*

The piano notes floated into the room, slow and melancholic and beautiful.

Darius walked back to the couch. He pulled the wool blanket up to his chin.

He closed his eyes.

He was alone. His wife was gone. His friend was in another house. His children were three thousand miles away.

He took a deep breath, inhaling the cedar, the smoke, and the silence.

"Okay," he whispered to the empty room. "Okay."

He was finally, terrifyingly, free and would leave tomorrow to tomorrow.

CHAPTER 12: THE QUIET REBELLION

The Fortress (Atlanta, 11:42 PM)

T he house above him was finally asleep. Darius knew the specific acoustic signature of his home's slumber. He heard the dishwasher cycle end with a muted chime. He heard the settling groan of the floorboards in the hallway as the temperature dropped. He heard the silence that only comes when Sasha finally puts her phone on the charger and stops broadcasting.

He sat in the Fortress, the leather of his chair cool against his back.

He hadn't turned on the main lights. The room was lit only by the low, rhythmic pulse of the server rack in the corner—blue, green, blue, green—and the glow of his laptop screen.

He wasn't working. There was no code to fix. The weather app he had built at the cabin was running flawlessly on a side monitor, logging wind speeds in a forest three thousand miles away.

Wind: 4 mph. Direction: NW.

He stared at that number. 4 mph. A gentle breeze. He could almost feel it. He could smell the damp earth and the cedar.

Here, the air was scrubbed and filtered. It smelled of ozone and expensive HVAC filters.

He felt a phantom vibration in his pocket—the ghost of a demand. But his phone was upstairs, face down on the nightstand.

He was alone. And for the first time since leaving the cabin, the aloneness didn't feel like freedom. It felt like a vacuum.

He opened the browser. **ProtonMail.**

The cursor blinked in the empty field of the login screen. It was a rhythmic taunt.

Log in, it seemed to say. *See if she's there. See if she's real.*

He hesitated.

The doubt, sharp and cold, pricked at him. What if the cabin was just a fever dream? What if Amara had gone back to Portland

and realized that "The Union" was just a coping mechanism for two middle-aged people having a breakdown? What if she was currently upstairs with Carter, laughing about the man who made wind-chime apps?

He looked at his hands. They looked like the hands of a tech executive again. Clean. Manicured. The dirt from the hike was gone.

He needed to know if the signal was still live.

He typed his password. It was long, complex, and uncrackable.

He hit **Enter**.

The Attic (Portland, 8:45 PM)

Three thousand miles away, the rain was doing the heavy lifting that the silence did in Atlanta.

Amara sat on the floor of the attic.

She had cleared a space near the dormer window, pushing aside boxes labeled "Keela: 2010-2012" and "Christmas Decor." She had dragged up the scratchy wool blanket from the cabin—the one she had "accidentally" packed in her tote bag.

It smelled like smoke. Real smoke. Not the *Exhale* candle sold on Instagram, but the kind of smoke that clings to your hair after you've sat by a fire and told the truth.

She wrapped it around her shoulders, pulling it tight.

Downstairs, the house was settling. The "Essay Crisis" had ended not with a bang, but with a whimper. Keela had eventually used Grammarly. Carter had eventually stopped hovering.

They had survived her boundaries.

But now, in the quiet, the doubt crept in.

She looked at the rain streaking the glass. It blurred the streetlights into smears of orange.

Did I imagine it? She wondered. *The ease? The laughter? The way I felt while painting?*

Re-entry was violent. The gravity of her old life was heavy, pulling at her skin, trying to drag her back into the shape of "Mom," "Wife," and "Dr. Lewis." It would be so easy to just... slide back. To pick up the tile samples. To edit the essay. To be the Utility.

She picked up her iPad. The screen was the only light in the attic.

She opened the browser. Incognito Mode.

She logged in.

The Signal

Darius saw the draft count change.

It didn't flash. It didn't ding. It just quietly ticked over.

Drafts (1).

The breath rushed out of his lungs. A knot in his chest, one he hadn't realized he was holding since he walked out of SeaTac, suddenly loosened.

She was there.

He clicked on the folder.

The subject line was simple.

Subject: Re: The Terms (Saved Draft)

He opened it.

The timestamp was from two minutes ago.

The line held, she had written.

I told them I was unavailable. The sky didn't fall. Carter burned the chicken, but nobody died. Keela used the spellcheck.

I'm sitting in the attic. It's cold, and there are spiders, but I have the blanket. The scratchy one.

I can still smell the fire.

Darius read the words twice. He traced the letters on the screen with his eyes. *The scratchy one.*

It was a small detail, a granular texture of their shared reality. It anchored him.

He positioned his hands over the keyboard. The mechanical keys felt different now—not like tools for work, but like an instrument.

He typed slowly.

I'm in the Fortress. The servers are loud tonight. Sasha is asleep.

I told her I was off the clock. She looked at me like I was speaking Aramaic. But then she just... pivoted.

He paused. He thought about the ring light. The frantic optimization of peace.

She bought a $400 blanket to compete with your wool one. She's trying to brand the silence.

But she left me alone.

He hit **Save**.

The Connection

In the attic, Amara watched the words appear.

She let out a soft, shaky laugh. The sound was swallowed by the insulation and the rain, but it felt real.

Brand the silence, she thought. *God, he's funny.*

She missed his humor. She missed the dry, cynical edge that cut through the noise of their lives. She missed the way he looked at her when he wasn't trying to fix anything.

She typed back.

Let her have the brand, Darius. We have the copyright.

I checked the wind speed on your app. 4 mph. It sounds peaceful.

I'm not running away anymore. I'm just staying still. But staying still is harder than running, isn't it?

She paused, her finger hovering over the screen.

Tell me it's real, she typed. *Tell me we didn't just hallucinate the last week.*

She saved it.

The Anchor

Darius saw the new lines.

Tell me it's real.

He swiveled his chair away from the screens. He looked into the shadows of the basement. He looked at the turntable in the corner, silent now.

He thought about the moment on the porch, the specific weight of her hand in his. He thought about the look on her face when she was painting—the smudge of blue on her cheekbone.

He turned back to the keyboard.

It's real, he typed. *It's the only real thing in this house.*

I kept the rental car receipt. I put it in the safe. Not for taxes. Just for proof.

We're doing it, Amara. We are minding our business.

Go to sleep. I'll see you in the quiet.

He hit **Save**.

The Sleep

Amara read the final line. *See you in the quiet.*

She closed the iPad. She pulled the wool blanket tighter, scratching her chin, feeling the roughness of it. It grounded her.

She wasn't just a mother hiding in an attic. She was a shareholder in a secret economy.

She stood up, her knees popping in the cold. She left the iPad hidden under the box of Christmas decor.

She walked downstairs. The house was dark. She could hear Carter snoring in the bedroom—a rhythmic, oblivious sound.

She walked into the bedroom. She didn't wake him. She didn't fix the cover he had kicked off.

She climbed into her side of the bed. She lay on her back, staring at the ceiling fan.

She closed her eyes.

She didn't count sheep. She counted wind chimes.

Bing. Bong.

She fell asleep before she reached ten.

In Atlanta, Darius closed his laptop. He didn't turn off the servers. He let them hum. They sounded different to him now—not like a cage, but like a heartbeat.

He walked upstairs. He brushed his teeth. He walked into the master bedroom.

Sasha was asleep, her silk eye mask firmly in place, blocking out the world she couldn't curate.

Darius climbed into bed. He lay still, listening to the silence of the house.

It wasn't empty silence anymore. It was populated.

He wasn't invisible. He was a man with a draft folder and a key to a cabin that didn't exist on any map he was willing to share.

And for the first time in twenty years, when he finally drifted off, he didn't dream of drowning in the data.

He dreamed of the lake.

CHAPTER 13: THE SHAREHOLDERS (EPILOGUE)

Part I: The Asset Class (Two Years Later)

The Olympic Peninsula didn't do "happy endings." It didn't do crescendos or fade-outs or triumphant swells of violins. It did fog. It did damp moss that clung to your boots like a needy lover. It did a silence so heavy, so specific, and so dense that it felt less like the absence of noise and more like a weighted blanket draped over the roof of the world.

On the porch of **Cabin Three**—a structure that did not exist on Airbnb, Zillow, or any map accessible to the general public—Darius and Amara sat in matching Adirondack chairs.

The chairs were teak. They were ridiculously expensive.

Dung-chul, the Golden Retriever who was arguably the CEO of this entire operation, lay between them. He was snoring with the rhythmic, wet rattle of a dog who had never known a day of cortisol in his life. His paws twitched, chasing a phantom squirrel through a dreamscape where he was always fast enough, and the squirrel was always slow enough to be caught but never eaten.

Darius held a ceramic mug of coffee with both hands. It was black. It was bitter. It was the temperature of molten lava.

He looked out at the lake. It was a flat, pewter sheet, undisturbed by the chaos of the world. The mist was lifting slowly, revealing the jagged line of the fir trees on the opposite bank like teeth being bared.

"You know," Darius said, breaking the silence not because he needed to fill it, but because the irony was too delicious to keep trapped in his own head. "I got a notification this morning. Sasha's 'Sereni-Tea' line just went global. She's shipping to Dubai."

Amara didn't open her eyes. She leaned back, her face tilted toward the weak, watery sun filtering through the clouds. She looked older than she had two years ago, but less eroded. The lines around her eyes were still there, but they were crinkle lines now, tracks left by laughter rather than stress fractures.

"Dubai," she mused, her voice low and scratchy with the specific, luxurious rasp of a woman who hadn't spoken for three hours. "We love a global scalability moment."

"She's selling a candle called 'The Keep Your Man Burn,'" Darius added, taking a slow sip, savoring the burn. "It smells like sandalwood, rain, and 'emotional availability.' It retails for eighty-five dollars."

Amara snorted—a loud, unladylike sound that made Dung-chul thump his tail once in protest at the disruption.

"That is my favorite part of the portfolio," she said, finally opening one eye to look at him. "The fact that your wife monetized our coping mechanism."

"It's not a coping mechanism," Darius corrected gently, turning the mug in his hands. "It's a subsidiary, he jokes."

They sat there, two majority shareholders in the most successful, secret corporation on the West Coast. They weren't hiding. They weren't running. They were simply... off the clock. Cabin Three was purchased by them a year ago. It's their hideaway.

And the best part? The truly dark, hilarious heart of the matter?

They hadn't stolen this peace. They hadn't lied for it.

Their spouses unknowingly had built the fence around it for them.

Part II: Monday Morning Audit

Monday morning in Atlanta did not arrive; it assaulted.

Darius walked into the glass-walled conference room on the 40th floor of the Resolute Tower at 8:58 AM. The air was pressurized, recycled, and freezing—kept at a temperature designed to keep biological organisms awake but uncomfortable. It smelled of ozone from overheating laptops, dry-erase markers, and the specific, yeasty despair of stale bagels.

The "Crisis Team" was already assembled, vibrating with caffeine and terror.

There was Brad (VP of Strategy), wearing a fleece vest that cost more than Darius's first car, sweating through his gingham shirt. There was Kevin (Junior Dev), currently hyperventilating into a can of Pamplemousse LaCroix. And there was Sheila (HR), sitting in the corner with a notepad, present solely to witness the murder.

"The server migration failed," Brad announced, slamming a manicured hand on the mahogany table. He looked at Darius like he was expecting him to drop to his knees and beg for mercy. "We are down, Darius. The client is screaming. The dashboard is red. It looks like a crime scene. What is your plan?"

Old Darius—Pre-Cabin Darius—would have felt the familiar acid spike of cortisol in his throat. He would have apologized. He would have promised to work through the night, trading his sleep for Brad's bonus.

New Darius—Shareholder Darius—felt nothing. Actually, that wasn't true. He felt a mild, anthropological curiosity.

He looked at Brad. He watched the vein throbbing in Brad's temple, a little worm of stress trying to escape. He looked out the window at the gray smog of the city, watching a hawk circle a skyscraper.

Darius pulled out his chair and sat down. He didn't open his laptop. The sound of the chair scraping against the floor was the loudest thing in the room.

"Good morning, Brad," Darius said. His voice was dangerously calm. It was a baritone rumble that belonged in a jazz club, not a panic room.

Brad blinked, his programming glitching. "Did you hear me? We are bleeding metrics!"

"I heard you," Darius said. He clasped his hands on the table, resting them on the cool wood. "You're shouting. It's bad for morale. It triggers Kevin."

Kevin let out a small, wet whimper behind his LaCroix can.

"And the migration failed," Darius continued, his voice smooth as bourbon, "because you insisted on launching it on a Sunday night with a skeleton crew to save four thousand dollars in overtime pay. I told you that in the email dated October 12th. I cc'd Sheila."

Sheila looked up, startled to be perceived. She nodded slowly.

"Excuse me?" Brad sputtered. "Are you... are you giving me attitude?"

"I'm giving you data," Darius said, leaning back. "Here is the plan. Kevin is going to roll back the update. I am going to authorize the overtime pay you denied last week, so the team actually logs on. And you are going to call the client and tell them we caught a critical bug and prevented a catastrophe."

"I can't tell them that!" Brad yelled, his face turning the color of a steamed ham. "That's a lie!"

"It's consulting," Darius corrected. "And it's the only way you keep the account."

He checked his watch. "I have a hard stop at five today, by the way. I have a board meeting."

"A board meeting?" Sheila asked, pen hovering. "With who? You don't sit on any boards."

Darius stood up. He smiled. It wasn't his usual "customer service" smile. It was a shark's smile—all teeth and no empathy.

"Personal board," he said. "Union Holdings. Very exclusive."

He walked out of the room. Behind him, he heard Brad whispering to Kevin, "Does he look taller to you? He looks taller."

Amara's Day

Three thousand miles away, in a rainfall-gray office in Portland, Amara was dealing with her own crisis.

The room smelled of expensive lavender oil and damp wool. Her 10:00 AM was "Jessica," a devastatingly wealthy woman whose primary trauma was that her life was too perfect, and she suspected the universe was gaslighting her.

"I just feel," Jessica sobbed, the sound grating like a drill against Amara's temples, "that my nanny judges me. When I ask her to cut the crusts off the organic bread, she does it, but she does it... aggressively. Do you know what I mean? It's a micro-aggression. It's Crust-Based hostility."

Old Amara—The Utility—would have leaned in. She would have validated. She would have exhausted herself trying to reframe Jessica's narcissism as "anxiety." She would have carried Jessica's water until her own back broke.

New Amara—The Shareholder—took a sip of her tea. It was Earl Grey. It tasted like bergamot and boundaries.

She looked at Jessica. She saw the designer tissues. She saw the diamond tennis bracelet shaking as Jessica wept over sandwich preparation.

"Jessica," Amara said.

Jessica looked up, hopeful for the enabling. "Yes?"

"That sounds exhausting," Amara said.

"It is! It's so—"

"For the nanny," Amara finished.

The air left the room. Jessica froze. "Excuse me?"

"I'm looking at your chart," Amara said, flipping a page she wasn't actually reading. "We've spent six sessions discussing the nanny's energy. We haven't spent any minutes discussing why you, a grown woman with a master's degree, are threatened by how a nineteen-year-old cuts bread."

Jessica's mouth opened. Then closed. Then opened again. "I... well, I pay you to support me."

"You pay me to help you grow," Amara corrected. "Growth is uncomfortable. If you want support, buy a body pillow. If you want to figure out why you need to control the crusts, stay in the chair."

Silence stretched in the room. It was heavy. It was the sound of a dynamic shifting, of the therapist stepping out of the role of 'Paid Friend' and into the role of 'Mirror.'

Amara waited. She didn't rush to fill the silence. She just sat there, radiant in her indifference to the tantrum.

"I think..." Jessica whispered, her voice smaller now, stripped of the performance. "I think I'm lonely."

"There we go," Amara said, closing the file with a satisfying *thud*. "Now we're working."

When the session ended, Amara walked Jessica to the door. Jessica looked shaken, but strangely relieved. She looked like someone who had finally hit a wall that didn't move.

Amara walked back to her desk. She opened her laptop. She opened a private browser window. She typed in a password.

DRAFTS (1)

She clicked it. A message from Darius, saved three minutes ago.

Subject: (No Subject) Body: I just told a VP to authorize overtime or learn to code. I think I might get fired. Or promoted. I don't care which. How goes the healing profession?

Amara smiled. Her fingers flew across the keys.

Body: I just told a client to buy a body pillow. We are dangerous. P.S. Don't get fired yet. We need to pay the property tax.

She clicked **SAVE**.

She closed the laptop. She spun her chair around to look at the rain falling on the city. She felt light. She felt invincible.

She finally understood what Darius meant. Minding your Black ass business wasn't just about ignoring the foolishness. It was about realizing that *you* were the business. And for the first time in twenty years, she was turning a profit.

The Brand (Atlanta)

The transition back to Atlanta was usually jarring—a shift from analog to digital—but now, it felt like walking onto a movie set where Darius was the director, not the prop.

The house in Buckhead had been repainted. The walls were no longer "Eggshell"; they were a shade called "Oat Milk," which looked exactly like Eggshell but cost twice as much per gallon because it sounded healthier.

Sasha stood in the center of the living room. She was adjusting her ring light, which hummed with a low, electric buzz—the mosquito of the modern age.

She looked tired. But it was an expensive, curated tired. She was wearing a beige loungewear set that cost more than Darius's first car, and her face was dewy with a serum made from flowers that only bloomed on Tuesday.

"Okay, guys," she whispered to her phone, putting on her 'Wellness Voice'—a pitch that was half-NPR, half-sedative. "Welcome back. Today we are talking about *parallel play* in marriage."

She gestured vaguely to the background, where Darius was sitting on the couch.

He wasn't hiding in the basement. He wasn't seething. He wasn't fixing a server.

He was just reading a book.

"See," Sasha continued, panning the camera slightly to include him in the frame. "Darius and I don't need to be glued at the hip to be connected. He has his quiet time. I have my platform. We are... distinct entities vibrating at different frequencies."

Darius looked up. He saw the lens staring at him like a cyclops' eye.

In the old days, the rage would have spiked. He would have felt used. He would have felt like content.

Now? He felt a strange, detached affection.

He smiled. It was a small, genuine smile. It was the smile of a man who knew exactly where his passport was, who knew the gate code to a cabin three thousand miles away, and who had a flight booked for Friday under the name of "Site Inspection."

"Hi, guys," Darius said calmly.

Sasha froze. Her hand wobbled. She hadn't expected the Prop to speak.

"Oh!" she recovered quickly, her smile widening to a blinding wattage. "He speaks! We love a supportive king. Drop a heart in the chat for Darius!"

She cut the feed. The ring light died. The room plunged back into normal, oat-milk colored reality.

Sasha's shoulders slumped immediately. She rubbed her temples, the "Wellness" mask dissolving into exhaustion.

"Was that okay?" she asked, her voice dropping the performance. "Did I sound authentic?"

Darius closed his book. He looked at his wife. He didn't see a monster. He saw a woman running a small business based on her own anxiety, trying to sell peace because she couldn't find it herself.

"You sounded great, Sash," he said gently. "You sold it."

"Good," she sighed, walking to the kitchen to pour a glass of wine. "Because the twins need cars. And your wallet is closed."

"It's a long-term investment," Darius said, suppressing a grin as he turned the page. "Growth takes time."

The Boundary (Portland)

In Portland, the revolution was quieter, but bloodier.

Amara stood in the kitchen. It was 6:00 PM on a Tuesday. The air smelled of burnt garlic—the signature scent of Carter trying to help.

Keela, now twenty-one and taking a 'gap year' that mostly involved critiquing Amara's grocery choices, walked in. She was wearing vintage overalls and looked like a disgruntled farmer.

"Mom," Keela said, dropping her bag on the counter. "I need you to edit my resume. I'm applying for a barista gig at the co-op, and it needs to sound... grounded."

"I'm cooking," Amara said. She didn't look up. She was chopping carrots with a rhythmic, meditative *thwack-thwack-thwack.*

"So?" Keela leaned against the counter, picking up a piece of carrot. "Multitask. You always multitask."

Amara put the knife down. She turned to her daughter.

She didn't yell. She didn't sigh. She channeled the energy of the Cabin. She summoned the spirit of the lake.

"Keela," Amara said pleasantly. "I am not a multitasker. I am a serial tasker. And right now, my serial number is occupied by carrots."

Keela blinked. She chewed the carrot slowly. "What does that even mean?"

"It means no," Amara said. "Use ChatGPT. Or ask your father. He's in the den looking over contracts."

Keela gasped. Her mother had gone off script. "You've changed. You used to be nicer but I understand."

"I used to be tired," Amara corrected, picking up the knife. "There's a difference."

Carter walked in then, holding a paint swatch in each hand. He looked harried, his forehead gleaming with the sweat of decision fatigue.

"Babe," he said. "Gray Mist or Pewter Calm? For the downstairs bath?"

Amara looked at the swatches. They were identical gray squares. They were the color of depression. They were the color of a waiting room in purgatory.

"Pick the one that makes you feel like you have a soul," Amara said, picking up her wine glass.

Carter stared at the swatches. He stared at his wife. "Uh... Pewter Calm?"

"Excellent choice," Amara said. "I'll be in the bath. Do not knock unless the house is on fire. And even then... check the extinguisher first."

She walked out. She didn't lock the bathroom door. She didn't have to. They knew better now. She had trained them, not with anger, but with absence.

The Shareholder Meeting (Present Day)

Back on the porch of Cabin Three, the sun was beginning to set. The light hit the water and shattered into a million pieces of copper and gold.

The wind picked up, rustling the hemlocks.

From the trees, a faint, melodic chime drifted toward them.

Bing. Bong.

Darius smiled. He closed his eyes. "The app is working."

"It's annoying," Amara said, but she leaned her head on his shoulder. "It sounds like a mindfulness app that won't shut up."

"It's data," Darius said. "It's wind speed converted to audio. It's poetry, Amara."

"It's noise," she said. "But I like it."

They sat in the silence that wasn't empty. It was filled with the specific, heavy comfort of being known.

They weren't having an affair. Affairs were frantic. Affairs were about escape. Affairs were about what you were missing.

This was residence. This was about what they had found.

"You ever think about the math?" Darius asked softly, watching a hawk circle the thermal currents above the lake.

"What math?"

"The hours. We spend three weeks there. One week here. But I feel like I live here. Like... the ratio is flipped in my head. My real life is the cabin. The rest is just the commute."

Amara nodded. She reached down and scratched Dung-chul behind the ears. The dog groaned in ecstasy, his leg kicking involuntarily.

"It's not about the hours, Darius," she said. "It's about the anchor. We know this exists. So when I'm standing in the kitchen and Keela is calling me a fascist for not buying almond milk, I'm not really there. I'm here."

"Dissociation?" Darius teased.

"Location independence," she corrected.

Darius laughed. He reached over and took her hand. His thumb traced the callus on her palm—a paint stain she hadn't scrubbed off from her morning session.

"We did it," he whispered. "We actually pulled it off."

"We formed an invisible LLC," Amara agreed. "We protected the asset."

"And the asset," Darius said, looking at her, "is us."

Amara smiled. She squeezed his hand.

"Meeting adjourned," she said.

Darius leaned back. He closed his eyes. He listened to the wind chimes sing the weather's song.

He wasn't a Prop. He wasn't a Utility.

He was half of the Chairman of the Board.

And business was good.

www.ingramcontent.com/pod-product-compliance
Lightning Source LLC
Chambersburg PA
CBHW050534260626
47157CB00004B/1592